ANTIOCH

Jessica Leonard

PMMP

Perpetual Motion Machine Publishing
Cibolo, Texas

Antioch
Copyright © 2020 Jessica Leonard

ISBN: 978-1-943720-49-1

www.PerpetualPublishing.com

Cover Art by Matthew Revert

PRAISE FOR
ANTIOCH

"*Antioch* is full of twists, dread, and the unsettling fog of ambiguity. You'll willingly follow Bess around her increasingly Gothic small town during a bizarre murder spree. Just watch your unsteady feet. A promising debut."

—Paul Tremblay,
author of *A Head Full of Ghosts*
and *Survivor Song*

"A realistic rendering of small-town frustrations leading to crime-solving aspirations. A young woman's dual obsessions with Amelia Earhart and shortwave radio draw her into a mystery surrounding a missing local woman and a sadistic serial killer. For anyone who enjoys films like *Zodiac*, true-crime books with shocking photos in the middle, and late-night conspiracy theorizing with friends, *Antioch* is a freaky fun dead-end town to visit."

—David James Keaton,
author of *Stealing Propeller Hats from the Dead*

PRAISE FOR ANTIOCH

"Antioch is full of twists, dread, and the unsettling fog of ambiguity. You'll willingly follow Bess around her increasingly Gothic small town during a bizarre murder spree. Just watch your unsteady feet. A promising debut."

—Paul Tremblay,
author of A Head Full of Ghosts
and Survivor Song

"A realistic rendering of small-town frustrations leading to crime-solving aspirations. A young woman's dual obsessions with Amelia Earhart and shortwave radio draw her into a mystery surrounding a missing local woman and a sadistic serial killer. For anyone who enjoys films like Zodiac, true-crime books with shocking photos in the middle, and late-night conspiracy theorizing with friends, Antioch is a treaty fun dead-end town to visit."

—David James Keaton,
author of Stealing Propeller Hats from the Dead

For Jonathan—keep reaching for the stars

BESS JACKSON LIVED in a small two-bedroom home with an open floorplan and an attached garage, which she'd originally purchased with a man. But that man wasn't around anymore. Which is, in more ways than one, how she found herself arriving home at night in a car belonging to someone entirely different. This new man was named Greg, and while he wasn't the first person she'd dated since she'd found herself the sole owner of her home, it still, years later, felt odd to be in this place with someone else.

"Should I walk you in?" Greg asked.

"You don't need to do that," Bess replied. The neighborhood was well-lit with houses that were a little too close to each other.

"Yeah, but maybe I should. I mean, you never know in Antioch. Vlad could be hiding in your coat closet. I'd better come in. Just to make sure you're safe."

Bess rolled her eyes and laughed; it was all a fun

1

joke. But there was enough truth behind the joke to make her accept the offer. The Impaler Murders began in Antioch nearly two years ago, and as brave as Bess liked to think she was, it made living alone a little more ominous sometimes. Two years was a long time to be afraid. It made a person weary.

Once inside, Greg made a show of looking under her couch for any murderers. Before she could stop him, he poked his head into the garage and called out to potential serial killers. But his joke—which was already stretched thin—seemed to snap entirely when he saw the garage.

"What's all this?" he asked.

"All this" was the overstatement of the year. Inside the garage there was only a lone card table, its top decorated with swipes of dust, a spiral bound notebook, and a pristine shortwave radio.

"That," Bess said with pride, "is my shortwave, a Grundig Satellit 750." She gazed lovingly at her radio, then at Greg with somewhat less admiration.

"What's it do?" Greg said, less a formal question and more of a "Why am I looking at a radio?" rhetorical.

As far as first dates went, this was not Bess's worst. Greg was handsome enough, although his precisely gelled blond hair and ample use of Axe body spray wasn't something Bess usually looked for in a man. He'd been mostly polite to her and while he didn't seem interested in her as a person, he had enough manners to try and fake it.

"It just, you know, listens. It searches." Shortwave as a hobby wasn't something easily explained. She wished he hadn't seen the radio. Having her head

2

impaled on a stick now seemed at least somewhat less exhausting than continuing a conversation with someone too polite to say they didn't care.

"Huh," Greg said, looking around at the empty white walls. The room had the musty smell of a dirt-floored cellar. She could tell he was sorry he'd offered to walk her in. He certainly hadn't foreseen hanging out in a gross, empty garage looking at a radio. "Have you been doing this long?"

"Since I was fifteen. My dad got me my first radio."

"Was it something you picked up from him?" Greg asked, and Bess heard the hope in his voice. Maybe it was a family thing. His family was into tennis, and perhaps her family preferred little radios.

"No," Bess said, her eyes on the floor, for some reason sorry to be disappointing him. "I had this Amelia Earhart obsession. That really got me going."

"Did she use one of these?"

"No, well, I mean, yeah, I guess maybe. But that wasn't it. Do you know much about her?"

"Earhart? She was a pilot who crashed. That's pretty much all my knowledge on the subject."

"Yeah, and that's basically it, but her disappearance is still a huge mystery. There are tons of theories about what happened to her. Some think she crashed into the ocean, but there are other people who think different." She glanced back at the radio, trying to decide how to continue. The more rational part of her brain told her not to continue at all. But goddammit, once she got on a roll about Earhart theories she couldn't help herself. A big part of her wanted to tell him everything even if he didn't care.

He wasn't going to stop her, and it was so rare to have a captive audience. "So, one of the theories says a girl heard transmissions from Amelia Earhart the night she went missing. She heard them on her shortwave radio, but no one believed her. She reported it to the coast guard back then, but they dismissed it right away. So that's kind of how it started for me. Learning about those transmissions."

"It's a conspiracy theory."

"I guess. But no one can for sure prove or disprove it."

"That's what a conspiracy theory is," Greg said.

"Okay, well, a conspiracy theory shaped my life."

Greg shrugged. "It happens." He stuck his hands in his pockets and walked to the radio. He pointed to a small glass ashtray sitting next to it. "Oh hey, fantastic. Do you mind if I . . . ."

"Knock yourself out," Bess said. It was the first time he'd alluded to being a smoker all night, and Bess wondered if this hidden vice accounted for all the Axe Body Spray.

Greg lit a cigarette from a pack he had hidden inside the inner pocket of his sports jacket and then tucked them away without offering one. "Tell me more. What does this girl hear on the radio?"

"She hears a lot of stuff. Things which later lead some people to think Amelia actually landed her plane off Gardner Island, but died there before she could be located or rescued."

"I've never heard of Gardner Island."

"It's called Nikumaroro now."

"I've heard of that even less." Greg took a long draw from his cigarette and exhaled away from Bess and the radio. Ever polite. "But I want to know the conspiracy. Give me the weird shit. You didn't get obsessed with radios for no reason. Not just because some girl said she maybe heard something neat once."

Bess tried to think of an easy way to tell the story. Every detail of Betty's notebook and the interpretations of what she claimed to hear was etched into Bess's brain, but how much of it was actually interesting? And why was she still interested in being interesting? She didn't have any real desire to ever see Greg again, but here she was, choosing her words carefully and trying to impress. Maybe she was polite too.

"Okay, so this girl, her name's Betty, she hears a transmission while she's cruising around on the shortwave and the voice says, 'This is Amelia Earhart.' And Betty always keeps a notebook with her while she's messing with the radio because you never know what you might hear and sometimes she wrote down song lyrics and stuff because she was fifteen and that's what kids do, I guess." Bess paused for breath and looked at Greg, who was smiling at her like she was adorable—not in an attractive way, more like in a pitying way. She forged ahead. "So she writes down everything she hears and when some people who knew a thing or two actually got ahold of the notebook a few decades later, and read the things she said, some of it started to make sense. And it led some people to Gardner."

"What parts made sense?"

"She wrote down 'N.Y.' a few times, which she later said was an abbreviation for New York City. Like, Earhart kept repeating New York City. Which doesn't make any sense. Except it does when you think about how Gardner is a coral atoll and right there along it is the wreck of the SS Norwich City. Norwich City was a steamer that ran aground there in 1929. The wreck was a hazard, everyone knew about it. If she could see it and she was trying to tell people where she was, it makes sense that maybe she was saying the name of the ship. Not New York City, but Norwich City. You see?"

"That's actually really interesting." Greg sounded impressed or surprised, Bess couldn't decide which. "Is there more?"

"There is, but it can take forever to really get into it, and I'm pretty tired." She gave the sheepish smile of the person who admits they're sleepy first. She'd purposely set their first date for a Wednesday night so she could easily use the excuse of getting to bed early for work the next day.

"Oh yeah, of course." He squashed out his cigarette in the ashtray. "I didn't mean to keep you up. Thanks for a nice night, Bess." Greg leaned in and kissed her on the cheek. He pointed to the table. "Is that notebook like Betty's?" He was gesturing to a small green notebook with a cheap ink pen Bess stole from a motel lying across it.

"Oh, gosh. Yeah, I guess it is. I like to write down stuff sometimes. When I can't sleep at night it helps me relax. I guess because it's basically mindless. It's like meditating. Instead of chanting or whatever, I write."

Greg smiled. "That's nice. I like that idea. I'll call you later, okay?"

Bess was positive this was a lie. "Should I walk you

back out now? You know, the Impaler . . . woooo," she made a low key ghost noise and wiggled her fingers ominously.

"Nah—I'm safe as safe can be, Bess. You know old Vlad only likes the ladies." Greg laughed. Bess gave a little smile to show she was a good sport, too well-mannered to let on that his comment unnerved her. She had never known a single one of Vlad the Impaler's six victims, but sometimes she had nightmares about them. In her dreams the six heads sat on her kitchen counter, all talking at once. Sometimes they spoke in different languages. Sometimes they made screeching noises so loud Bess would have to cover her ears. As she tried to decipher what they were telling her, a large shadow would appear in the doorway. The heads would fall silent. She could never understand what they were saying.

Once Greg's car had pulled away from her house, Bess changed into blue pajama pants and an old white tee shirt. There was a full six pack of Fat Tire waiting in the fridge. She opened one with the tulip-shaped bottle opener that hung from her wall and took a few swallows before retreating to the worn charcoal grey couch and turning on the television. She flipped through the channels too quickly to register what was on any of them, then scrolled through again, slower this time, trying to pay attention.

Bess stopped on the local news. She thought back to Greg telling her he'd better walk her in so Vlad didn't get her. There hadn't been a new victim in months. She didn't know if she would be more relieved to hear nothing on the news, or to hear they'd found his next victim—head spiked onto a PVC pipe in some abandoned lot in Antioch, body never to be found. If they found someone else she could feel safe for a couple of months.

Bess shook her head and changed the channel, lingering on an old episode of *MythBusters* before giving up and switching it off entirely. Restless energy twitched through her limbs. The beer was on her coffee table and she plucked it up and gulped some down before replacing it and closing her eyes, allowing her mind to wander.

The repetitive caw of seagulls filled her ears. Bess pictured Amelia Earhart out there in the ocean with her injured navigator, Fred Noonan. Fred slipping in and out of lucidity, yelling for his wife and trying to run out of the plane and into the ocean. The rising tide lapping into the Lockheed Electra. She smelled the salt air and saw the black profile of the Norwich City like a hole punched into an already dark sky.

"This is Amelia Earhart."

Frantic SOS signals sent out to possibly no one. Everything had gone so wrong and now her legacy would sink into this one tragic failure.

Where would she have gone? Bess wondered if she drowned straight away—her legs scraped and cut by jagged bits of coral, her muscles too exhausted to carry her to shore—or if she made it to the beach before dying of exposure, starvation, or dehydration. Giant coconut crabs would carry away her body bit by bit. The ocean would overtake her plane. Her existence would be erased.

Bess played each scenario out in her mind.

ANTIOCH

Sometimes Noonan was with her, sometimes not. Sometimes she watched him drown as he raved and fought against the ocean.

Her eyes popped open. Her body was damp with sweat. She'd fallen asleep. At first she thought she'd been dreaming about Vlad but then it came back to her.

Amelia.

After Earhart's disappearance, rumors started to spread that she'd been captured by the Japanese. At the time, any English-speaking women broadcasting Japanese propaganda were known as "Tokyo Rose", and some theorized one of the women on the radio might be Earhart. Her husband, George Putnam, investigated these rumors diligently. He listened to hours of recordings, but he never heard his wife's voice.

Bess breathed deep and reached for her beer. It was warm and a little flat, but Bess gulped it down as fast as she could. She stood and tried to stretch out the kink that had settled into her shoulders. For a second, she considered going to bed but knew she would never get back to sleep.

The garage always felt a little too warm for most people, but Bess thought the temperature was perfect. Dragging a folding chair over from the corner of the room, she settled herself at the card table. She clicked the radio on and slowly scanned through the channels, pausing here and there, moving backward, trying to pick up a strong signal.

With a meticulous hand she wrote the date at the top of a fresh page in her notebook. Jotting down bits and pieces she found interesting as she went, Bess began her nightly meditation. She switched between the upper and lower sideband setting to hear random voice communications. Sometimes she would linger over the beep-screeches of data signals, letting the noise overtake her, thinking about how it was so senseless to the ear—to someone who didn't know better—but with the right programs it could be translated. The noises were her religious chants. She wrote down weather conditions being broadcast to pilots over the ocean, collected international news reports alongside song lyrics.

She closed her eyes and listened in awe to the foreign language broadcasts, the words like a prayer she couldn't quite understand but found comfort in. From time to time she listened in on truckers and ham radio operators talking back and forth. She especially liked hearing people use Morse code. It was something she learned in her early twenties, and while she missed some things, she'd learned enough universal abbreviations that she could catch the drift of the secrets people were sharing. Women were referred to as "YL", meaning Young Lady, and men were "OM", Old Man—this was an old language, a gallant one. 88 meant "love and kisses".

Then there was the Buzzer. Tonight seemed like a Buzzer kind of night. Bess tuned her receiver to frequency 4625 kHz. A dull endless hum filled the garage. It was legendary in the shortwave world, a Russian station that had been playing this same monotonous tone since the early 80's, occasionally joined by a low deep foghorn-like sound. Maybe once a week there would be a word or two in Russian.

After about an hour of buzzing her nerves were

calm and her mind was easy. Her eyelids began to droop but she didn't want to leave the radio. To go into the quiet house would be to give her imagination free reign once again. The station drowned out her dreams.

This is Amelia Earhart
This is Amelia Earhart

Bess jerked awake. A page of her notebook was stuck to her cheek and came up with her head before gravity caught on to what was happening and yanked the book back to the table.

SOS
SOS

Bess observed the radio, unsure if the transmissions were real or following her out of her dreams.

I can feel it

It wasn't a dream. Someone was broadcasting an SOS message across the shortwave frequencies. Quickly, Bess snatched up her pen and scribbled down the last line of the message and waited.

Intel

Intel? Was this some sort of military broadcast? Those were usually encrypted. Much of the modern world had moved on from the shortwave for sensitive communications, but if this was a true distress call there was no telling who it may or may not be.

Intel here

At this point a second voice rang out, farther away but loud.

Margaret! Margaret!

Chills ran through Bess's body. There was a pause before the first voice resumed. The words were garbled, the beginnings being cut off or lost completely. The signal was weak, but Bess was afraid to adjust the radio for fear of losing it altogether.

. . . since feast day
It's rising now
Bevington
Bevington
. . . find buddy

Bess wrote as fast as she could, desperately trying to get down as much of the message as possible.

SOS
SOS
Can you hear?

The second voice once again called for Margaret. But then something else. It sounded like the word "dragging." From far away she heard a man yelling to Margaret about dragging something. Or that

12

something was dragging. Maybe Margaret was dragging. It was too hard to make out.

Intel here

The original woman spoke again, this time in a hushed tone like a stage whisper.

Tell her
Tell her
Tell Her

There was another long pause. Either the transmission ended or the signal was entirely lost. She laid down her pen and stared at it, hearing only static. And then:

This is Amelia Earhart

The clicky buzz-hum of radio static hung heavy in the muggy, unairconditioned garage. Bess breathed deep through her mouth and let the late August humidity coat the inside of her throat. She looked down at her notebook. Her chicken scratch shorthand looked back at her. Capital E, squiggle line, lowercase t.

She continued with the deep, slow breaths until her heart slowed from a thud to an insistent knock. Reaching with measured, deliberate motions, Bess clicked off her radio. The longer she examined what she'd written, the more obvious it became—someone was fucking with her.

"Very funny," she said to no one, or maybe the room.

Someone wanted to play a trick on her.

"But how did they know what frequency I'd be on?"

The room did not answer, but rather presented her with more questions.

Who would play a trick on you? Who would care enough? No one knows you.

"I guess Greg knew about the Earhart stuff."

Only what you told him.

"Even Carrie White got pranked."

Carrie was more popular than you.

"I'm a fucking adult. I don't need to be popular."

The room did not answer, but instead kept a sort of smug silence. Its point had been made. This transmission probably wasn't directed at Bess.

But that didn't mean it wasn't a hoax, it was just one being played on someone else. Bess hearing it was like when someone in a crowd waves at someone behind you. And you *think* they're waving at you, so you wave back . . .

If it was a prank, why wouldn't they recite the real Earhart transmission? Betty's notebook pages detailing the possible last transmissions of Earhart are online—scanned and transcribed with annotations—for the world to see. So what would be the purpose of altering the message? Unless that repeated line, "Intel," meant this was some sort of code.

Anyone acquainted with Earhart theories would catch some familiar phrases in there. Like "Bevington." Eric Bevington was a Cadet Officer at the British Gilbert and Ellice Islands Colony. Three months after Earhart disappeared, he snapped an infamous photo just off the west end of Gardner

Island. Some claim to see signs of what might be the landing gear of a Lockheed Electra poking out above the water. The black, burnt-out remains of the SS Norwich City lolls in the background. Bevington and his photo fit into the Earhart mythos, but not into her transmissions.

"Unless it was a ghost," Bess said, trying out the words to see how they sounded. The notion that Amelia Earhart's ghost had reached out to her through a shortwave radio seemed at least somewhat unlikely.

She looked at the notebook. The SOS was undeniable. Someone needed help. Someone named Amelia Earhart. Or possibly Margaret. And there it was again. Like Bevington, Margaret was close, but not quite right.

In Betty's notebook, where she transcribed what she believed to be transmissions from Earhart, there are several references to a man—presumably navigator Fred Noonan—shouting the name Marie over and over. Which doesn't mean anything until you take a minute to consider that Noonan's wife was named Mary Bea, and then you have to wonder. Marie. Mary Bea. New York City. Norwich City.

Not Margaret.

But *close*.

Bess thrust her thin fingers into her dark mass of curly hair and massaged the sides of her head. There was no clock in the garage but she knew it must be early morning. Her knees cracked when she stood. The bright white notebook paper glared up at her. She turned her back on it.

Inside the house proper, Bess trudged down her

short hallway and into the bedroom. The floor was spattered with dirty clothes and shoes—a dropping off station rather than a lived-in space. She flopped diagonally across the bed and was asleep within minutes, sinking into the hard, dreamless sleep of the dead.

2

THE PHONE WAS RINGING. Bess blinked against the hot sunlight coming through her window. Her arm shot out and groped for her cell phone. No luck. The ringing was coming from the living room and she stumbled out, arms stretched in front of her like a barrier, to retrieve it.

"'Lo?"

"Bess?"

"Yeah?"

"Where in the holy fuck are you?"

"I'm here. What?" Bess rubbed her eyes and looked around the house, confused.

"You are supposed to be *here*. Should, in fact, have been here two hours ago. I've been trying to call you all morning, Bess."

Bess finally recognized her boss's voice. "Oh shit, Carol, I'm so sorry. Look, I didn't hear the phone. I don't know what happened. I had a long night."

"You were fooling with the radio again." It wasn't a question. Carol knew. This wasn't the first time a

17

bout of insomnia and late-night shortwave made Bess late for work.

"It was different this time, Carol. Something kind of weird happened. Look, I'll be there really soon. Just let me get dressed. I'm sorry."

"Forget it. Take the day off. Get some rest. But you'd better not forget our Friday meeting."

Carol hung up before Bess could apologize again.

Bess laid the phone down and glanced over at the clock. It was ten forty-two. For a few moments she didn't move at all, just stood there and let her mind be blank. The temptation to lay down and sleep was overwhelming, but she knew she'd be awake all night if she did.

Bess had been the assistant manager of Antioch's only locally owned bookstore, The Rabbit Hole, for three years. Carol Liddle was the shop owner. Books weren't an easy sell these days, but Carol had managed to not only stay in business but expand. Last year she'd added on a bar serving a small rotation of craft beers and doubled her sales. In addition to the drinks and books, The Hole also specialized in book-related merchandise like tee shirts, tote bags, and coffee mugs. In the digital age, bookstores had to be savvy. By making her store a gift shop and hangout, Carol had beaten the odds.

"What am I doing?" Bess asked aloud.

The room hummed.

Bess ambled into the kitchen to make coffee. The coffee was in a canister on the top shelf of the refrigerator. Someone had once told her coffee stayed fresher if you refrigerated it, and while Bess no longer knew who'd told her that or had any idea if it were true, she still did it out of habit. So much of her home life had become just that: habit. When she moved in, there were coat hooks on the wall next to the front door—so that was where she hung her coat.

With half a pot brewing, she padded into the garage and grabbed her notebook. She sat at a small dining room table outside the kitchen and flipped open the notebook, the sounds of percolation filling the room with warm inhabited noises.

She read back over the SOS message and lingered over the phrases that stood out to her. The coffee pot beeped and she poured a cup and carried it to the table.

Intel here
Margaret, Margaret
Since feast day

Feast day. Last night she hadn't paid any attention to the words, but in the light of day they suddenly struck her as important. Who had said them? Was it the man who was yelling "Margaret," or the woman who called herself Amelia? She couldn't remember and cursed herself for not taking better notes. The wheels in her mind were turning almost too fast for her to keep up. Then something clicked.

Bess stood abruptly and strode to her computer, tucked snug on a tiny desk against the half wall that served as a bridge between her kitchen and living room. She jiggled the mouse until the screen brightened and she could bring up a search engine.

Margaret Feast Day
ENTER

Bess studied her search results.

- St. *Margaret of Scotland—Saints & Angels—*
  Catholic Online
- St. *Margaret of Antioch—Saints & Angels—*
  Catholic Online
- St. *Margaret Mary Alacoque—Saints & Angels—*
  Catholic Online

St. Margaret of Antioch. If any of this meant anything—and it might not—her instincts were telling her to follow the connections. She clicked on the link for St. Margaret of Antioch. X-ing out of a pop-up box asking her if she wanted to subscribe to a Catholic newsletter, Bess quickly scanned the page.

At the top, in a grey box labeled "Facts," she saw Margaret's Feast Day was July 20th and she was the patron saint of childbirth, pregnant women, dying people, kidney disease, peasants, exiles, and the falsely accused. Margaret served a diverse crowd. She was, like so many of the old saints, a martyr.

"'Margaret is one of the Fourteen Holy Helpers, and she spoke to St. Joan of Arc.' Impressive. I don't know what a Holy Helper is, but still . . . impressive."

A sudden noise made Bess shriek. Her head whipped in the direction of the front door. It was the doorbell. She waited a moment to see if they would knock or ring the bell again. The room was silent. While she wasn't expecting anyone, it wasn't necessarily a call for alarm just because someone stopped by. And yet Bess's heart was racing and she found herself praying whoever it was would go away. Company wasn't something she was accustomed to, not since she started living alone, and something about unexpected guests felt menacing.

ANTIOCH

Bess crept over to the door and tentatively opened it a crack. No one was there. Breathing a sigh of relief, Bess opened the door wider and stepped out onto her front stoop. She scanned the street for a UPS truck or neighbor but saw neither.

"Kids . . . " she said absently, although it was the middle of the day on a Thursday.

Bess closed the door and walked back to her desk where she grabbed a Post-It Note from the top drawer and jotted down the words, "July twenty." That was over a month ago. Bess's mind reached back, searching for anything of importance that might have happened a month ago, but came back empty. She herself had probably spent a sleepless night alone in front of her radio inventing a reason to still be awake. Briefly it crossed her mind that she was giving this too much thought because she needed it to be more exciting than it was. She needed something. But she pushed the thought away so quickly it was as if it had never occurred.

She retrieved the notebook and her coffee cup and brought them to the desk. Bess closed her eyes and thought about last night's broadcast. She heard the man's voice shouting in the distance and chills ran down her arms. She pictured Fred Noonan struggling to escape the sinking cockpit of his plane, shouting his wife's name for comfort, for posterity, for rescue.

The transmission last night had said something about rising water. Or had it? No, that's what Bess (wanted it to be) thought it was. All the message last night had said was, "it's rising." "It" could mean anything—water, smoke, Satan.

The phone cut into her thoughts. This was the most calls she'd received in ages.

"Hello?"

"Hey, Bess, it's me, Carol."

"Oh, hey."

"Look, I feel a little bad about earlier. I shouldn't have gotten so mad."

"Are you joking? You had every right to be mad at me. I was stupid."

"You were." Carol paused and Bess heard her breathing into the phone. "I'm worried about you, Bess."

"What? No, come on. I'm fine."

"No, you clearly aren't. You never go out—"

"I literally *just* went out last night."

"What? With whom?"

"His name's Greg."

"Fantastic. Tell me about him. Something other than a name."

Bess sighed and thought for a moment. "He was . . . polite. Taller than me, blonde hair."

"So, a polite white man of average height?"

"I'd say that sums him up fairly well."

"And how did it go?"

"Amazing. We're getting married tomorrow."

"Well, this is the first I'm hearing about it. You didn't tell me you were going out with anyone."

"That's because it wasn't any of your business."

"Bess, I want you to listen to me," Carol said. "I'm being serious right now. You stay inside all the time with that radio. You never sleep. You're an old cat lady without any cats."

"Are you saying I should get a cat?"

"At least then there'd be someone to eat you when you died."

"At least."

"I know I'm only your boss, and you can tell me to fuck off if you want, but I know you. I know you probably better than anyone—which, by the way, doesn't say much for your social life. I want you to be okay." Carol was silent and Bess knew this was the part where she was supposed to agree or cry or both. This was when she was expected to comply.

"I will be," Bess said. She waited for Carol to say something else, but the line remained quiet. "Hey, do you want me to come in? I can close for you."

"Actually, that would be nice. I could use a night off."

"For sure. I'll be there within the hour. Who else is working?"

Carol had already hung up.

Bess entered The Hole an hour later. Lucy was behind the bar, wiping the glossy countertop with a clean white rag.

"Somebody's in trou-ble," Lucy sing-songed, her eyes dancing with a gossip's delight.

"Mind your business." Bess glanced over to see who else was present. There were no patrons seated at the little six-stool bar and, for once, Bess was grateful. "Don't you have something better to do than wait on zero customers?"

"When you aren't here, I have to bartend, so don't blame me."

Bess snorted at the idea of "bartending." The Hole didn't serve liquor, only beer, and they had a whopping three taps to complement the four or five canned and bottled options they offered. It was more difficult to make drinks at Starbucks.

"Is Carol still here?" Bess asked.

"In her office, as usual." Lucy hitched her thumb toward the back of the store.

To get to Carol's office you had to go all the way to the back of the shop and up a short flight of stairs to reach what the staff referred to as "the Rabbit's Loft." The loft looked out over the store by way of a long picture window. Carol's desk faced the window—a vigilant overseer and micromanager.

"I hope you aren't giving Lucy any shit," Carol said as Bess walked in.

"I wouldn't dream of it."

"You better get used to her. She isn't going anywhere. In fact, if I retire, she'll probably be your assistant manager."

"If you leave me this store I'll fire that peppy little Becky in a heartbeat."

"No can do, her job security would be a condition of your management, same as Wayne's. I've hand-picked these people and they'll stay as long as they like."

"I don't know why we're talking about it. You'll die in this store and we all know it."

"It's true. I'm trying to plan it out so as to get the most possible drama. I can't decide if I should leave a trail of clues to my corpse or try to expire in a crawlspace and haunt the new releases." A smile creased the stoic façade of Carol's face.

ANTIOCH

"Sounds like you have a full night of planning. You should get going."

"Lucy's here until close. Wayne will be here in about an hour to cover the floor."

"Once Wayne gets here I'll send Lucy home," Bess said, trying to suppress her own smile.

"No way. This might surprise you, but most people go to bars at night. You'll need her. At least I hope you do."

"Okay, you win, I'll see you tomorrow."

Bess wandered down to the sales floor, which was just as dead as the bar. But then, Thursday afternoons weren't notoriously busy at any store. Bess took the free time to wander over to the religious section and skim the titles for something involving saints. Carol purposely shunned most Christian books, saying that Antioch had plenty of them already and would benefit more from something outside what could be found in every church pew in town. Bess saw that *The Handmaid's Tale* was the newest employee pick in the section and smiled.

Finally, her eyes settled on a book titled *Saints, Sexism, and Sinners: Eve Was Framed*. After searching the table of contents, Bess skipped to chapter seven: "Imaginary Saints and the Warnings They Gave Us". Margaret of Antioch only received one short paragraph.

As with most stories, this one begins with a dude wanting to fuck. In this case the dude is Olybrius and the hole he wanted to fill belonged to Margaret of Antioch. Margaret spurned his advances and was righteously punished. That punishment came in the form of beheading.

Beheading was a popular theme in Antioch these days. Bess couldn't speak to the filling of holes. The story didn't quite align with anything Bess knew of Amelia Earhart, but she still felt like it had something to do with the message she'd heard the night before.

"You find Jesus?" a voice cut into her thoughts. Bess looked up and saw Wayne, his eyes on the book in her hands.

"Hardly," Bess laughed, putting the book back on the shelf. "You know me, never found a book I didn't like."

"Well, I'm on the clock if you've got something better to be doing. Or if you want to keep on reading about Jesus."

"I wasn't reading about Jesus," Bess said. Wayne was a nice man, but he had the tendency to take a joke too far. He'd probably still be talking about Jesus next month, like he was trying to force an inside joke out of casual happenings. He was older than Bess, with short hair that had become mostly grey over the three years Bess had known him, and his dark brown skin had deep creases around the eyes from years of laughing at cheesy jokes and fake smiling at customers.

"You can play cool if you want, but I know what I saw." Wayne dropped a wink at her. "That does remind me, though. You know my church has a young adult Bible study I think you'd really like."

"Wayne, I love you, but I haven't been to church since I was twelve."

"Sure, sure. But I think you might like it. Other young people. It's a nice social time."

"I appreciate the offer."

"Okay, okay. You don't have to tell me twice. I won't pester you about it." But he remained next to her.

"What's up, Wayne? You look like the cat that swallowed the canary."

"I heard through the grapevine that you had a date last night, young lady."

"And I assume the grapevine is named Carol?" Bess asked, rolling her eyes.

"Lucy *and* Carol, actually." He leaned in like Brutus to the senators.

"You're all a bunch of gossiping church ladies."

"So, who is this mystery man? Carol said he's white."

"His name is Greg. And what the fuck?"

"Now Bess, didn't your father ever tell you not to date a white boy?" Wayne asked, looking stern and playful all at once.

"As a matter of fact, he did. And if I didn't listen to him, what makes you think I'm going to listen to a nosey old bookseller?"

Wayne laughed and clapped her on the back. "I guess you won't listen. Now, don't get all bent out of shape. I was just trying to pull your leg a little."

"Well, my leg's tired. Now if you don't mind, I've had enough talk about my love life at work to last me for the rest of the year." Bess was smiling even though she didn't feel much like it. She didn't like her personal business on display at her job. It wasn't professional. The last thing she needed was for Wayne to call her dad and start discussing the men she was seeing. Bess and her father didn't speak much. If she thought too much about it, it made her sad. They'd been close once. Bess's mother died of pancreatic cancer when she was in college and things had never really been the same. He resented Bess for being away and Bess hated him for trying to hold her back. Their relationship devolved into strained birthday phone calls and Christmas morning breakfasts.

Bess wandered back up to the office and sat behind the small, cluttered, wooden secretary desk she claimed as her own. From one of the shelves she pulled a pocket notebook and opened it to a clean page. After thinking a moment, she wrote a small list: *Margaret of Antioch, Beheaded, Feast Day, July 20.*

Thus far most of her clues were inferences and giant assumptions. Taking the notebook with her, Bess headed back out to the floor. There was plenty for her to be doing in the office, but she couldn't focus.

A blond man sat at the bar now, facing away from Bess. Where in the fuck was Lucy? She picked up her pace. Something about the man was familiar.

"Sorry about your wait, what can I get you?" Bess asked the man.

"Bess!" he said. "I was hoping you'd be here."

"Greg?" she asked, but it was more shock than question. "What are you doing here?"

"I came to see you, of course."

"How did you know I worked here?"

"You told me. Last night." His smiled faded for a second before reemerging, confident, as if it had never faltered.

"I don't think I did."

"I thought I'd stop in, surprise you," Greg said, his attention fully on Bess. "I had a really nice time last night."

"You did?" Bess asked in genuine confusion.

"I did."

"Well, I guess I'm flattered. Do you maybe want a drink? Or is this a social call?" She was suddenly grateful that Lucy had disappeared. The last thing she wanted was an audience. Or Lucy having a window into her private life.

"Sure, I'd love a drink. What's good?"

"Uh, what do you like? IPA? Stout? Lager?"

Greg considered for a moment. "It's too hot out for dark beer. How about an IPA?"

"You're in luck. We just tapped this Deschutes Fresh Squeezed IPA. It's sort of citrusy."

"Sounds good to me. Thanks." He accepted the beer and sipped it tentatively. "I can't really stay long, but I did want to come by, tell you I had a nice time." He reached for his wallet but Bess waved at him.

"This one's on me. And, it was really great of you to stop by, but I've got to get back to work. It was nice to see you, though." Bess gave him her practiced customer service smile.

"Oh sure," Greg said, standing. "You know, I should go. I'll call you later, okay?"

"Absolutely. But you didn't even finish your drink."

Greg was already out the door.

"The fuck is this?" Lucy said, coming up next to her and pointing to the full beer.

"We had a customer. Where the hell were you?"

"I had to pee. We really had someone come in and leave in the time I was back there? And they didn't even finish their drink?"

"We really did, yes. Next time make sure someone else is up here to cover before you leave."

29

Bess walked off with the beer in hand.

"Seriously?" Lucy called after her.

"What? He didn't take a single sip. You think I should pour it out?"

"Not my business . . ."

"You're right, none of it is."

If Greg actually did call her, she planned to let him know his presence in her bookstore was not appreciated. She'd worked her ass off to be seen as an authority figure here, to be respected. All this focus on who she dated made her seem childish.

Bess closed up the store that night and, as usual, was the last to leave. The Rabbit Hole didn't have its own parking lot, but there was a small free community lot across the street that customers and employees used. It was shared with patrons from the other businesses on the block as well, with the exception of Pat's Deli on the corner, which had its own private lot.

The streetlights kicked on before the sun set and by the time it was full dark the area was washed in soft orange light and long, slender shadows. Bess's sneakers scuffed across the pavement. She'd parked her white 2007 Oldsmobile Aurora in the farthest corner of the lot. Her cell phone was in one hand, her car keys in the other. The keys poked out through her fingers like little daggers, ready to punch holes into anyone foolish enough to sneak up behind her. It was a habit she'd picked up in college when late-night walks across campus were the norm.

She was only ten feet from her car when she noticed a white paper stuck under her windshield wiper. Unlike the occasional takeout menus left there,

ANTIOCH

this appeared to be a fully blank piece of paper, it wasn't even folded. Bess approached it slowly, scanning the lot for anything out of the ordinary, a person, a car, perhaps a large stack of papers.

Gingerly, she reached out and plucked the paper from her windshield. On the opposite side, in careful block letters: JULY 20.

"Feast Day," Bess whispered.

THE DOOR HAD barely closed behind her and already Bess had kicked her shoes off and hung her purse on a hook. She headed straight for her computer, pulled up a search engine and typed: *July 20*

The results were not encouraging.

International Chess Day, Moon Day, Nap Day, National Fortune Cookie Day, National Lollipop Day . . .

This wasn't working. Goddamn mysterious notes with their goddamn cryptic bullshit. She leaned back in her desk chair and closed her eyes. Taking a few deep breaths, Bess tried to calm her mind and focus on the facts.

Someone knew she'd received that transmission last night. And the note on her car validated her connection between the words in the transmission and Margaret of Antioch's feast day. But Bess wasn't sure if she should be nervous about the mysterious note, or someone's apparent knowledge of the

ANTIOCH

message she'd received. Every question she asked herself led to more and more questions. The only thing certain was that someone asked for help last night, and maybe it meant she was an idiot, but she intended to try and help.

When Bess heard her phone ringing she opened her eyes and reached for it.

"Hello?" she asked.

Nothing but silence on the other end. She rolled her eyes. Telemarketers waiting for her to say hello a second time before launching into their pitch. Instead, she hung up.

Turning her attention back to the computer, she tried a different search.

Antioch News July 20

There it was. The sort of headline she didn't know she'd been looking for: *Local Girl Still Missing*.

Bess clicked the headline and read.

Antioch police are still searching for a local woman reported missing on July 20th. Amy Eckhardt went missing after driving her red '03 Dodge Neon to a local store for dog food. Her roommate, Monica Bortles, called police when Amy still hadn't returned home the next morning.

The Sheriff's Office is in search of any information that could lead them to find Amy. She is described to be 5'07", 145lbs., with strawberry blonde hair and blue eyes.

If you have any information on

Eckhardt's whereabouts, contact Detective Scott Howland at 270-555-2307.

Bess read the article a second time.

New York City. Norwich City. Marie. Mary Bea. Amelia Earhart. Amy Eckhardt.

So maybe a ghost hadn't contacted her after all.

Bess's mouth felt very dry, so she retrieved a bottle of water from the fridge. She took a long swig, but immediately choked on it when her doorbell rang. Leaning forward, she hacked spit-mingled water onto the carpet, gasping for air.

"The fuck?" she managed. The door blurred as she squinted at it through tear-filled eyes. Dizzy from the coughing, she walked over and got up on her tiptoes to peek through the decorative glass embedded at the top. She couldn't see anyone, although her field of vision was pretty limited. Maybe her choking scared whoever it was away.

Bess poked her thin neck out the door and looked around. The light from her neighbor's porch illuminated most of her yard and the lamplight streaming through her own front windows cast crooked shadows across the porch. She closed the door once again and turned the lock.

The melodic ring of her cell phone cut through the room.

Her heart thudded in her chest. She rushed to the phone and snatched it up.

"Hello?"

Silence.

"Carol? Is that you?"

ANTIOCH

The voice on the other end was almost too soft to be a whisper. It was well-articulated wind. "It's not Carol."

Bess's eyes filled with tears and she bit back the scream that fought its way up her throat.

"Amy?"

A long screeching wail cut through the line. Bess winced and pulled the phone away from her ear.

"MARGARET!" The shrieking noise sounded neither male nor female. It was the sound of agony and rage made pure and given voice. "You be good now, MARGARET!"

"Who is this?" Bess screamed into the receiver.

Silence.

And then the whisper: "Find me, Bess."

There was a roar—or maybe more of a ferocious gurgle—and the line died.

Bess dropped the phone. Her hands clasped at her chest as if to catch her heart before it could escape. Her mouth was open, but no sounds made their way out.

The doorbell rang again. Bess collapsed on the carpet. This time the bell did not stop after one chime. It kept on. Someone was out there holding the button down. Her knees shook as she stood. One trembling step at a time, she went again to the door. Her fingers touched the knob just as the ringing cut off. Bess jerked her hand back and counted slowly to ten before turning the lock and pulling it open.

As before, the stoop was vacant. But there was something in the yard.

To the right of the steps, stuck down in what would have been landscaping if Bess ever had the gumption to tend her yard. That's where she saw the dark shriveled head impaled on a bright white PVC pipe.

Her own head felt warm and numb. Without thinking, Bess stepped out toward the head. It was deformed. The eyes had been removed. Empty sockets glared at nothing. The rest of the face seemed misshapen. The skin was burnt black and deeply lined.

The sagging, terrible head slipped to the left as her fingers grazed its side, felt the soft, flimsy rubber. A mask. Not a head at all, but a dragon mask over a pipe stuck in her yard.

Inside, the phone was ringing.

Bess carried the mask in with her and dropped it just inside the house. She relocked the door and ran to where the phone lay, discarded on the carpet.

"What the fuck are you playing at?" she asked.

"I said I'd call. I'm calling."

Bess knew this voice. She stayed quiet, trying to sort everything out.

"Helllllloooo? Bess, are you still with me? It's Greg."

"Greg?"

"Yeah. Hey, is everything okay?"

"No. I can't talk to you right now."

"Okay." Greg paused. "Sorry I bothered you. You be good now."

"What?"

"What?"

"Tell me what you just said and why you said it."

"I didn't say anything. I said I was sorry to bother you. I said to take care."

ANTIOCH

"That is not what you said." Her voice was a deep, thick tremble. Tears slid steadily down her cheeks.

"I don't know . . . Are you okay?"

"Don't call this number again." Bess hung up.

The phone immediately rang, but Bess hit ignore. She turned the sound off and watched the screen light up, "Unknown Number" scrolling across the display.

The doorbell rang, but only for a second. It was replaced by a soft knock, low on the door, as if someone were rapping with their hands down to their sides or maybe on their knees. The knocks migrated slowly to her right, the unseen visitor moving along the side of her house, knocking lightly against the siding as they went. When the knocking approached the living room picture windows, Bess had the urge to run over and close the blinds and curtains, to block out whatever might appear there. The knocking continued. But now it was more like a tapping as it beat across the window—the distinct sound of knuckles against glass. And yet, Bess saw no one. Goosebumps broke out across her arms. Her phone screen remained dark. She quickly called 911.

A male operator answered, "911, what's your emergency?"

"There's someone here," Bess croaked.

"What's that? Where are you? Is there someone in your residence?"

"No, they're . . . trying to break in. Please, send someone."

No response.

"Hello? Are you there?"

"Are you sure they want in?" The voice was

distinct and clear in Bess's ear. No background noise. "Maybe they want you to come out."

Bess looked down at the phone. The knocking stopped. The silence in the room amplified, making her ears ring.

"Go outside, Margaret," the voice on the other end shrieked. Bess ended the call and held down the power button.

She picked up the rubber dragon mask. It felt damp, but maybe that was her imagination, or a sensory deception based on the cool slick rubber. Bess slowly turned the lock and opened the front door just far enough to stick her hand through. She tossed the mask out into the night and slammed it shut behind her. Within seconds a deafening machine-gun knock reverberated through the house.

Bess pushed her back against the door to brace against the pounding and tried to catch her breath. Her hands shook. The knocks leached into her mind, short-circuiting her thoughts.

All the windows in the living room left too much liability, she was too easy to see, they were too easy to break, she was too easy to find. If only the knocking would stop so she could concentrate. Then an idea came to her. Slowly she raised herself to a crouching position and rushed toward the garage. She slammed the door behind her and looked around for something to barricade it. It locked, but from the inside. Grabbing the metal folding chair away from the radio table, she wedged it under the knob like she'd seen countless people do in movies. The only other way in or out was through the electric garage door and she'd kept that bolted shut ever since she stopped storing her car inside.

ANTIOCH

The sounds from the living room were muffled out there, but still audible. She stood in front of her radio, looking down on it as if it were holy. Soft static filled the space as soon as she clicked it on, further drowning out any noises from outside.

The floor was cold and hard against her butt as she lowered herself onto the ground. She couldn't reach the radio from down there, but that was okay. The static was enough.

A sharp pain shot from the middle of Bess's back up through her neck. She'd fallen asleep in the garage and her spine wasn't thrilled about it. Something had drawn her out of her sleep, and that thing was nagging at her mind now, telling her to be alert.

Someone was knocking on the front door.

She had no idea what time it was. Standing gingerly, she stretched her neck—testing the muscles—rolling it from side to side. The moment she opened the garage door, bright sunlight poured in through the windows.

Someone was still knocking, but unlike last night, this knock didn't seem so terrible. Nothing ever did in the morning. She cracked the door open. There stood Carol in all her corporeal glory.

"Let me in."

"Hey." Bess smiled and waved at her boss. She'd barely gotten the door open before Carol was fully through it. "What's up?"

"It's Friday," Carol said. "I've been out here for ten minutes." She seemed grumpier than usual.

"Jesus Christ, Carol. I was in the bathroom." She didn't know why she'd lied, it just felt right.

"Are you ready to go?"

"Go?" Bess asked, trying to make her mind accept that this was her reality—not a disembodied knock at her door and ghosts on her radio.

"Fuck, Bess. It's Friday! Manager's meeting. Are you suddenly new?"

Bess sighed. She'd forgotten their weekly meeting. They'd been having lunch at the same place every Friday for the last two years. Maybe she *was* losing her mind. No. She was under stress, not sleeping well. This wasn't her fault. Not this time.

"I know what day it is," Bess said. "Let me get my shoes on."

Carol drove. She wouldn't let anyone drive her anywhere. Bess assumed it was some sort of motion sickness issue, but she knew it could have just as easily been Carol's complete inability to give up control. Bess stared out the window at the scenery moving past them. Same old Antioch. Same old businesses.

"Hey," Bess said, something new catching her eye. "I didn't realize we had a historical society."

"Hm? Oh. It's been here forever. It's easy to overlook. They have a nice gift shop."

"What kinds of gifts?" Bess asked, amused.

"I don't know. Magnets, probably."

"You think it's a magnet shop?"

"Shut up. I have no idea. I just know they have a damned gift shop."

ANTIOCH

Bess smiled at her reflection in the glass. "What sort of information is in there? Do you know?"

"Historical stuff. I'm certain of that."

"Brilliant. Probably things about the founding of the town, right? Say, do you know why they call this place Antioch?"

"Are you kidding? Where's your head today? Why do they call anything anything? Why do they call Pittsburg Pittsburg?"

"It's named after William Pitt."

"You made that up." Carol was exasperated. She hated trivia.

"I didn't. Pittsburgh was named by General Forbes, in honor of William Pitt, Earl of Chatham."

They arrived at a small diner named Aunties. Bess would order a burger and a Coke. Carol would get a grilled chicken salad—dressing on the side—then complain about how good the burger smelled and how fat she was getting. It was a routine, but damn it, sometimes routines were real nice. Sometimes they could be the absolute nicest.

They spent the first few minutes going over the weekly sales numbers. Carol would be pessimistic and it was Bess's role to play the optimist.

"I made a bad buy with those fancy journals. They aren't moving," Carol said. She was holding a binder and checking off items as they discussed them, her left hand holding her light auburn curls out of her eyes.

"I don't think it's fair to call it a bad buy yet. We've only had those two months. Give it six, then we'll see."

"Has it really only been two months? It feels like longer. They're not as cute as I wanted them to be. I

41

think you're the only person who's bought one. And you get an employee discount."

"I like journals. Other people will, too." Bess bit into her burger and chewed slowly, thinking. "Carol?" she asked around a mouthful of half-chewed beef.

"Yeah?"

Bess swallowed hard and sipped her Coke. "Do you know about that missing girl? Amy Eckhardt?"

"Where's this coming from?"

Bess shrugged.

"No, not really. I mean, I heard a girl was missing. But I didn't know her."

"Do you think she was kidnapped? You know, like the other women?"

"I have no idea. Can we drop this? I'd rather talk about the historical society."

Bess had effectively ended the meeting then and there. The two of them finished their lunch and Carol paid the check, keeping the receipt carefully tucked into her wallet so she'd have it for tax season.

Once they were in the car, Carol turned to Bess, a stern look on her face. "I need to know you're okay."

"I'm okay." Bess smiled, rolling her eyes.

"I'm not kidding. You've been in another world lately. More than usual. I depend on you, Bess. If you need some time off, let me know. You have plenty of vacation time. I don't want you to burn out on me."

"I promise I'm okay." She buckled her seatbelt rather than make eye contact. "Hey, I might take you up on the vacation. But not right now. I'm sorry about being late. I'll do better." Bess smiled her brightest I'm-a-former-pageant-queen smile and hoped it was more convincing than it felt.

ANTIOCH

Carol didn't look persuaded, but she did start the car and back out of her parking space, which was good enough for Bess. On the way home, Bess again noticed the historical society, a small stone building that had probably once been a residence. It brought to mind the word "cottage." If any place in town would know the origins of Antioch, that was the place.

4

ONCE SHE WAS safely locked in her home, Bess thought over what she knew. She'd found some basic facts on St. Margaret of Antioch, but nothing that told her where to find Amy or even where to begin looking. And now she knew about the historical society. It had 'historical' in the name, but Bess would have sworn it was brand-new, a building where there had once been an empty lot popping up overnight to confuse her.

There was something she was missing. Something between St. Margaret of Antioch, the city of Antioch, Amy, and maybe even Amelia Earhart.

Checking her watch, it was nearing three, and she hoped the historical society would still be open. Bess quickly checked for a website but didn't find one. A quick look in the bathroom mirror told her she looked good enough for the historians and their gift shop.

Bess peered out her living room window, scanning the yard for any unusual people or masks. Possibly saints. The sound of a car driving past made her heart beat faster and she opened the door only enough to slip out then relocked it behind her. She hustled to her car and locked the doors before getting the key in the ignition. The afternoon sunlight created shadow monsters where there usually were none.

There was plenty of street parking in front of the Historical Society. Bess scampered up the cobblestone walkway to the door just as a small elderly woman was coming out.

"Hey there!" Bess called. The woman whipped her head around, startled, and held up her hands as if to block Bess or ward off the devil. Maybe she thought it was one and the same.

"I'm closing," the woman said in a voice that sounded like she thought Bess might be hard of hearing.

"Oh, that can't be," Bess replied, not sure what she meant.

"We are." The woman was brash, lacking the practiced customer service tone those in business unconsciously developed with time.

"You're kidding."

The woman eyed her warily. "Why would I make a joke like that? Do you think I don't know the time?"

"No, ma'am, I guess I'm the one who doesn't. I don't honestly know what time you close. I've never been here and was hoping you might still be here awhile."

"A while?" the woman asked.

"Yeah."

"What were you here after? The gift shop?"

"No, I was just needing to get some information about the town. Mostly how it began. How it got its name."

There was a long silence as the woman regarded Bess with steady bright green eyes. "Are you from the news?" she finally asked. It wasn't a strange question. Each time a new body was discovered in Antioch the 24-hour news stations would setup camp around town, looking for soundbites. Usually within a week they'd pack up and move to the next disaster, bringing fresh panic and fear to their audiences as an offering to appease the gods of news as entertainment.

"No, I'm no one," Bess said, hating how honest the words sounded. "I'm just interested."

"Not many young folk like yourself come around asking about such. And you're not a detective? One of those plain clothes types?"

"No. Why would I be?"

The woman turned back to the door. "No reason you should be. Why don't you come inside? It's nicer in here."

There was a small foyer inside, and the gift shop was to the right. Bess immediately noticed a tall fixture full of magnets. To the left was another small room decorated to look like an old-fashioned living room with large backed chairs and a small piano. A dark red velvet rope draped across its entryway gave it the resemblance of a museum. Farther back, the place was wide open and lined with bookshelves. A narrow staircase, adorned with another velvet rope, led up and out of sight.

The woman locked the door behind them and smiled at Bess before poking out a tiny but confident hand. "My name is Winnie Tate. It's nice to meet you."

"Bess Jackson."

"Okay then, Bess Jackson, what can I do for you this evening?"

"Well, I hate to be a bother. I'm wondering about the founding of Antioch. More than just the year."

"I think I can help you with that." Winnie shuffled into the main room then veered toward one of the bookshelves to the left, although she didn't actually pick up any of the books. Perhaps she liked the ambiance. "The current historical society had to do a lot of the research on its own. Antioch isn't mentioned in academic histories of the area. Any book you find on the matter will be written directly by one of our members. Past or present." Bess noticed the pride in Winnie's voice.

"If there aren't books about it, how did your members find the information?" Bess asked.

"Oh, dear, there were many a way to learn before the internet, you know."

Bess waited for more, but Winnie seemed to think this was explanation enough.

Bess shrugged. "Well then my main question is, how did the town get its name?"

"Antioch?"

"Er, yes."

"Antioch used to be Roman. What I mean to say is, it's the name of a Roman city. But it fell in 1268. Saint Luke was from Antioch."

"Which one was Luke?"

"Luke. You know: Matthew, Mark, *Luke*, and John? He also wrote Acts," Winnie said, as if she were imparting a juicy bit of gossip.

"So that's what the city of Antioch is named after?"

"No, not really. You have to understand, the

founders of Antioch had never visited Turkey. They didn't know one place from the other."

"I thought you said it was in Rome," Bess said. Winnie was talking fast and Bess was struggling to keep up.

"Right, well. It's Turkey *now*. Back then it was part of the Roman Empire. And later Byzantine, Ottoman . . . now it's Turkey. Can I go on?"

"Of course, I'm sorry," said Bess, not entirely sure why she was sorry.

"So yes, they never travelled to the area. And so they didn't really know the difference between, say, Antioch and Antioch in Pisidia. Although they *are* different places. So I suppose the correct answer is that Antioch is *fictional*. Which is to say, it wasn't named after a real place so much as an *idea* of a place."

"That's interesting," Bess lied.

"But it's not what you want to hear, right?"

"It's not that. I guess I was hoping there would be some neat story about the name."

"Well, I didn't say there wasn't. I just said it wasn't named for a specific place. You see, Antioch isn't really the name of the town at all."

Bess got the impression Winnie loved an audience. She was building her story with all the flair of a seasoned performer. Bess only smiled and waited for the show to continue. It was clear that audience participation was not required for this part of the act.

"No, no. You see," Winnie continued, "the name on the books is Margaret of Antioch. Mostly no one knows that, and to be sure, it's a rather long and awkward name for a town, so over the years the place was shortened to Antioch."

ANTIOCH

Bess's breath caught in her throat.

Margaret.

Winnie was eyeing her, perhaps with concern, but that didn't seem right; it was more like interest. Maybe amusement. She was watching to see what Bess would do. For the first time since entering the small historical society building, Bess felt her senses go on high alert. This old woman knew more than she was letting on, and if she had tried to distract Bess with fast talk about the Roman Empire and Turkey, it had worked like a charm.

"What are you here after, Bess Jackson?"

"A history lesson." Her eyes slid over to the locked entrance.

"You know about the dragon, don't you?"

Bess's thoughts fled back to the rubber dragon mask she'd found impaled at her doorstep only a few hours before. "I don't think I understand."

"Maybe you don't. But maybe you're starting to," Winnie said, a smile spreading out across her face, making some of the creases in her thin flesh deeper and some smoother.

"What's the dragon?" Bess asked.

"Margaret. Saint Margaret of Antioch. She's the saint of a great many things, but her greatest feat is, debatably, when she was eaten by a dragon and survived." Winnie's eyes were wide and dancing. "You're sure you're no reporter?"

"No, ma'am."

"I keep waiting for those bastards to catch on," Winnie said, almost to herself. Then to Bess, "Olybrius ordered Margaret killed. She was swallowed whole and yet she lived."

49

"And then she was beheaded," Bess said, filling in with what she'd read at the bookstore.

"Exactly so, Bess Jackson. Jonah lived in a whale. Margaret lived in a dragon. Nobody lives without a head. Not in Antioch. Not anywhere."

A chill shuddered through Bess. She kept her eyes on Winnie and focused on her breathing—easy, even breaths. "I should probably get back home. I've already kept you past closing, and I don't want to be out after dark. I appreciate your help." She was afraid of this old woman, or maybe just of what she had to say, but a definite sense of foreboding had claimed the room.

"Of course. I'm only the town historian, dear. Nothing sinister. But when your job is to watch and make a record, you tend to notice things others don't. Feel free to come back. I'm always here."

"Thank you." Bess had already backed most of the way to the doorway and when she turned, the closeness of the entry startled her all over again. She found the deadbolt and let herself out.

Back on the sidewalk she tried to make sense of what she'd been told. There was something off about the building's dimensions compared to what she'd seen inside. Something about the cottage didn't sit right with her. Then she realized there didn't appear to be a second story to the building at all. Walking to the side she craned her neck to try and see if there was an addition in the back, invisible from the front of the structure. Bess couldn't see anything. The uneasiness that now lived inside of Bess crept up a notch. She needed to get home.

The sky was soft and purple by the time Bess

reached her house. She scampered inside and dashed straight to the fridge for a beer. She knew she shouldn't be drinking. If she was sober it would be harder for people to paint her as a lunatic if she told them what was happening. But damned if that old woman hadn't made her nervous.

She took a long pull from her drink and returned to the safety of her garage. The radio was still on, static dancing through the empty spaces, reverberating against the walls and back to her. Was there a dragon swimming in all that noise?

Some people believe the Japanese shot down Amelia Earhart's plane and captured her. The story goes that the Japanese believed she was an American spy and she was imprisoned. Some say Earhart was beheaded at Garapan Prison, others that she simply died of dysentery. Either way, she met her end in a prison.

Bess allowed her mind to linger on images of Amy Eckhardt alone and dying either of dysentery or beheading. She thought about the dragon mask at her doorstep, and Winnie's story of Saint Margaret being swallowed whole but surviving. Amy could still live, crawl out of the dragon's throat, being mindful of the teeth around her neck as she went.

Bess pictured Earhart's head—short hair, empty eyes—rolling across the muddy ground, and then in a flash, she saw it again, not rolling, but spiked.

"Vlad the Impaler," Bess said. She was certain now.

The radio screeched in response. Bess sat up straight and strained to hear. For an instant, she thought she heard a woman calling. She reached for the radio and coaxed the knobs into giving up the transmission.

This is Amelia Earhart

Only now Bess knew better, not Amelia. It had never been Amelia.

This is Amy Eckhardt
SOS
SOS
Bevington Rising
Bevington
SOS
This is Amy Eckhardt
Intel near

But again, it wasn't "intel." Never had been.

Impaler
It's the Dragon
Please, anyone
I'm going to die in this basement

Even the soft background static cut out.
Dead.

Bess ran into her living room and frantically grabbed her cell phone.

It immediately started ringing in her hand.

"Hello?" Bess croaked into the phone.

"Hey Bess, it's Greg. I feel like things took an odd turn the last time we spoke and, well, I've been thinking about you a lot."

"Why?"

There was no answer.

ANTIOCH

"Greg?"

"I think we should talk. Can I come over?"

"This isn't a good time," Bess yelled at the phone and hastily pressed the giant red END CALL button.

She rummaged through notes on her desk about Catholic mythology and serial killers until she found the phone number she was looking for. It rang twice before a polite female voice answered.

"Hello, my name is Bess Jackson. I'm calling for Detective Scott Howland. I have information about Amy Eckhardt."

Bess sat alone in front of a cluttered grey metal desk and looked at her hands. She'd been waiting for the detective for about fifteen minutes and the longer she waited the stupider she felt. What could she possibly tell this man that he would care about or listen to? Cold, familiar panic rose in her chest and she dug into a hangnail on her left index finger and sucked the blood as it welled along the cuticle line.

Detective Howland let himself in and shook her hand. He was handsome by Antioch standards, probably forty, but his skin had seen enough sun during his life to make him seem older—the deep lines next to his brown eyes weren't so much from smiling as they were from squinting into harsh daylight. His hair was a medium brown, made lighter with age. He had a tall, lean body and as he strode over to sit in the chair opposite Bess, she noted the jeans he wore with his button down shirt and wondered if he thought he was a cowboy.

"Good afternoon, Miss Jackson," he said, a pleasant smile forming on his face and melting away, all in one motion. "I hear you're having a bad day."

"I'm not sure that's how I'd put it."

"Well, how would you put it?" His voice had the hard graceless accent of someone who spent too much time trying not to have an accent.

"I told them when I called last night. I think I have information about Amy Eckhardt."

"Right, and this is based on something you heard when you were listening to the radio?" the detective asked.

"Not exactly." Her face burned.

"What, exactly, is it based on, Miss Jackson? You've got my attention, tell me everything." His eyes locked, unwavering, on hers.

"I have a shortwave radio," she mumbled. "I heard an SOS message and the person said their name was Amy Eckhart."

"Miss Jackson, I'm sure you understand there are a lot of pranks involved with this sort of investigation. People like to fool about." He waved his left hand absently. "They try to scare nice young ladies like yourself."

"Are you investigating the Impaler murders as well?"

Detective Howland blinked. His head instantly straightened from the side-cocked "I'm a skilled listener" pose to the alert, detail-gathering position of an investigator. "Well, Miss Jackson, Antioch is a small town. We sometimes have to work on more than one case at a time."

"Do you think they're related? Amy and the Impaler?"

54

Howland sighed and eased back in his chair. "I see. At home playing armchair detective, are we?"

"I know about the dragon," Bess said.

There was a long silence. "What exactly is it you think you know, Miss Jackson?" He leaned in and Bess caught a whiff of cologne or aftershave, something distinctly masculine that made her heart race.

"I overheard a distress transmission from Amy Eckhardt. Then someone left a dragon mask spiked in my lawn. I heard another transmission and she said, 'It's the Dragon.'"

"Why didn't you call us after the first message? Or the mask?"

"I didn't really understand the first message. I didn't know what they were saying, not for sure. And the mask, well, it's like you said, it seemed like a prank. But the message last night was clear."

The detective considered what she'd said, his eyes studying her face. His gaze made her feel exposed and the exposure made her fidget. "When you called last night you gave them a rundown of the transmission you received," Howland said, handing Bess a piece of paper. "This is a transcript of what you told them. Would you mind looking over that and telling me if it still seems accurate?"

Bess studied her words for a minute. "Yes. This is it, as best as I can remember."

"You didn't mention any dragons in there."

"I'm sorry, I must have forgotten. I was upset."

"But they definitely said something about a dragon? Can you be specific?"

Bess closed her eyes and thought back. "She said, 'Impaler. It's the Dragon'."

Howland nodded, his eyes lost in thought. "Can you think of any reason someone would leave a mask like that in your yard?"

"I really can't. I mind my business, Detective Howland."

"I'm sure you do. I'm just trying to make sense of all this."

"Saint Margaret of Antioch was swallowed by a dragon," Bess blurted. Her hands shot to her mouth, trying to trap the words, or maybe shove them back into her throat before he heard them.

"Come again?" Howland asked. He seemed even more confused.

"Saint Margaret of Antioch," she said, her voice quieter now. "The town was named for her. She was swallowed by a dragon and survived."

"That doesn't sound entirely factual, Miss Jackson." He rubbed his hand across his face, his eyebrows knitted together. "Where'd you hear that? About a saint?"

"I, uh, from the historical society."

Detective Howland laughed. It was so unexpected it forced a startled cackle from Bess as well. "You mean to tell me, that you heard a mysterious SOS message and you went to the historical society?" His face changed when he laughed and Bess saw that he was more handsome than she'd originally given him credit for.

"It made more sense at the time," she said.

"I want to be very clear, Miss Jackson. The Antioch Police Department does not require the Scooby Gang running around town solving its mysteries. For your own safety, you should leave the detecting to the professionals." He paused and that charming grin snuck its way back onto his face. "But I suppose as long as you're not getting any more harrowing than the old ladies at the society, you'll probably be okay." She'd been on to something with the dragon, but the talk about Saint Margaret had ruined it. The interest he'd been showing her moments before seemed to fade away.

"Someone left that mask at my doorstep," Bess reminded him.

"True. Did you bring it with you today? We could check it for fingerprints." He said it like an afterthought. An empty gesture to make her feel better.

Bess sighed. "No, I threw it back out in the yard and it was gone the next morning." She shrugged and tried not to get angry when he again laughed.

"You know," he said, "it really was probably kids playing a joke on you. Now, who did you say you spoke with down at the good old historical society?"

"I didn't," Bess said.

"Could you? Please, ma'am?"

"Her name was Winnie Tate. She asked me if I was a detective."

"Well, that's real fine."

"I'm right about the dragon, aren't I?"

"I don't know what you mean, Miss Jackson. But if we find anything about the person who left a Halloween mask on your stoop, we'll be sure to give you a call. We greatly appreciate the hundreds and hundreds of tips the fine citizens of Antioch have provided to us over the last couple a years, and we document every single one." He tapped his finger against a manilla file folder to emphasize his point. "It's been real nice talking to you today, but I'm afraid I have a lot of work to do." He stood up, signaling it was time for Bess to do the same.

She didn't take the hint. "She said she was going to die in a basement. If I were you, I'd check houses with basements."

"We'll get right on top of that." Detective Howland's smile never wavered.

Bess stood to leave. She wanted to say more, to shake him and make him listen to her. Then she pictured the headlines: *Officer Attacked by Deranged Black Woman*. She'd be gunned down in self-defense and the world would hear about her overdue library books and how she hadn't been reliable at work lately. She gazed up at his practiced smile and eyes that crinkled up at the corners and tried to decide if he was one of the good guys.

"I only want to help," Bess said.

"I know you do, Miss Jackson. I really do. I appreciate your report and the time you took to come down here. And I do promise, we're looking into everything, but there's only so much collaborating I can do with a citizen such as yourself. If you remember anything else, feel free to call."

"I bet you say that to all the girls."

"Only if I really mean it."

Back at home, Bess took a hot shower. She always thought more clearly in the shower. She didn't know if she trusted Scott Howland to find Amy Eckhart. After all, Amy had reached out to Bess—not the police. Bess couldn't ignore her.

She popped a bag of popcorn in the microwave

and munched on it absently as she studied her notebook, wiping artificial butter on her pajama pants before turning the pages. There had to be some unexplored avenue to travel down. She re-read the article about Amy's disappearance and realized there was an obvious source of untapped information right in front of her. Amy had a roommate: Monica Bortles. If she could talk to Monica, maybe she'd know something about the disappearance, the dragon, or both.

Bess logged in to Facebook and searched for Monica Bortles. A short list of women popped up on the screen. The first one on the list shared five mutual friends with Bess and also lived in Antioch. Bess clicked the "About" tab on her profile and spotted her cell phone number, right out for the world to see. Either Monica hadn't gotten much publicity from her roommate's disappearance, or she enjoyed it. Either way, Bess considered it a lucky break. She dialed the number and waited, already rehearsing what she would say if the voicemail picked up.

Three rings and then, "Hello?"

"Hello, is this Monica Bortles?" Bess asked.

"Who's this?"

"I was calling about your roommate. To see if you could give me some information."

"Seriously? I've told you guys everything I know."

"I know it's frustrating, Miss Bortles," Bess said, trying to sound as poised and practiced as Detective Howland had in his office hours earlier. "But as we learn new information, sometimes there are questions we didn't know to ask before."

"New information?" Monica's voice on the other

end sounded painfully hopeful. It hurt Bess's heart to hear the optimism.

"Yes, well, did Amy ever say anything to you about a, uh, a dragon?" Bess faltered and realized she should have planned this out. Made a script. She sounded like an idiot.

"A what?"

"Well, a dragon. Did she have any friends with that nickname, I mean. Or, ah. Does it ring a bell at all?" Bess asked.

"Not really. Amy and me, I wouldn't say we knew a lot of people with nicknames. If that makes sense. We were in a book club, you know?"

"Is there anything at all you can tell me, something that maybe didn't occur to you before? Any new friends she'd made?"

"I really don't think there's anything else I can tell you. I'm sorry. I don't know what to say." There was a soft snuffling noise on the other end of the line and Bess realized she'd made the girl cry.

"I'm sorry, I won't bother you anymore," Bess said before hanging up.

Bess had a sinking feeling in the pit of her stomach. She wasn't going to help anyone by harassing the victims. She felt very small.

The phone rang in her hand and she answered it. "Hello?"

"Hi. This is Monica Bortles again. I remembered something." Monica sounded strange on the other end, distant, like she'd suddenly developed a cold within the last minute, or was doing an impression of herself.

"Oh, that's great. What did you remember?"

ANTIOCH

Bess barely had the words out before Monica interrupted her. "Amy had a boyfriend you should talk to. His name is Greg Leeds."

The name sent chills through Bess. "Thank you," she said and hung up the phone before Monica could say more.

The room seemed to close in around her and she hugged her knees in toward her chest, making herself smaller. He'd been inside her house. The phone calls, the visit to her work, it all took on a sinister glow in her memory. If he'd never seen the radio, would any of this be happening?

Greg wanted to talk to her. Maybe she should give him the opportunity.

Bess dialed the phone again.

"Hello?"

"It's Bess."

"Bess! Holy shit, are you okay? I tried to call you. I've been worried," Greg said.

"Tell me about Amy Eckhardt, Greg."

There was a long pause. Bess heard his steady breathing through the phone. She opened her mouth to ask again, when he finally spoke. "I think we should meet up. Talk."

"I don't know if that's such a good idea," Bess said.

"There are things you need to know."

"Did you put the mask in my yard?"

"What mask?"

"The dragon mask, Greg. The dragon!"

"Shit," Greg hissed. "What's been happening? Has anyone contacted you?"

"Where's Amy?" Bess asked.

"Goddammit, I don't know," Greg yelled. "Please,"

he said, regaining his composure. "Please, let me come over. We need to talk."

"You can't come here. Meet me. Meet me tomorrow, at the historical society." It was the first place that popped into her mind and she regretted it immediately.

"Fine, great," said Greg. "What time?"

"They close early. Better make it around one."

She hung up the phone without another word. Padding into the kitchen she picked up a bag of Dove Promises from the mottled blue countertop. The blue was there when she moved in and she'd commented to the realtor that she'd replace them first thing. Those counters would be the first to go. And yet here they were, five years later, as dull and blue as ever. She unwrapped a chocolate and popped it in her mouth. All the wrappers had little sayings on the inside, many of which had apparently been submitted by loyal Dove chocolate consumers.

Live, Love, Dove!—Tricia K. Indiana

"Sounds like something a person from Indiana would say," Bess thought, not truly knowing what she meant. But it felt true. Had she even been to Indiana? Perhaps once, as a child, on a road trip to some other location. Certainly never on purpose. Certainly never stopping there.

Wadding up the wrapper, she tossed it into the trash.

5

BESS LEFT THE house armed with her cell phone and a small pink canister of pepper spray. She'd called Carol the night before and told her she'd changed her mind—she *did* want to take a couple vacation days. She couldn't concentrate on work, not when so much was going on. Growing up, Bess thought nothing bad could ever happen in Antioch. It was too small, too isolated from all the chaos of the rest of the world. But someone was trying to prove that a small town could hold just as much evil as any other.

Bess intentionally arrived at the historical society at twelve thirty, hoping to get there before Greg. She parked as close as possible so her car alarm could be set off if needed, not that anyone paid attention to car alarms. The illusion of control set her mind at ease.

The front door was unlocked this time and no one stopped Bess as she entered the small foyer, grateful to escape the humidity. It felt like a storm was coming on. She drifted into the gift shop, looking for a good place to set up camp and wait for Greg.

"Your friend was here earlier," said a voice from behind her. Bess turned and saw Winnie, her face stern.

"What friend?"

"The detective. I thought you said you weren't with the police. Are the reporters on their way next?" Winnie's jaw was clenched, her bright eyes now hard green stones.

"Wait—Detective Howland was here? What did he want?"

"To ask if I spoke with you. I told him I had, but only about historical matters. He had a few of his own questions about the founding of Antioch. Seems to have some of his facts confused."

"He treated me like I was insane when I spoke with him. Why would he come here?"

"Maybe you invited him," said a man's voice to her right. Bess jumped, her heart zipping up into her throat. Greg was leaning against a wall in the foyer, arms crossed. His hair didn't have the stiff gelled appearance it did on their date. Instead, there was the distinctive greasy look of someone who hasn't showered in a couple of days.

"Can I expect the reporters soon?" Winnie asked again.

"No, Winnie, no reporters," Bess said. "This is Greg Leeds. With two E's." Bess emphasized the spelling, hoping Winnie would be able to remember this detail for the police, in case she turned up missing like Amy.

"Technically, it's three E's if you count the one in 'Greg,'" Greg said.

"Who's Greg Leeds?" Winnie asked.

ANTIOCH

"What do you know about Amy?" Bess asked Greg.

"Excuse me? You called *me*. What do *you* know about her?"

"Amy Eckhardt?" Winnie asked.

They both looked at her, but Winnie's eyes were only on Bess. "What do *you* know about Amy Eckhardt, Bess Jackson? Is that what the detective was in here about?"

"Greg was dating Amy," Bess said.

Greg's eyes were darting around the room like he expected the place to be crowded. Taking a look around herself, Bess saw they were apparently alone. Just them and a hundred Antioch magnets and keychains. "Look, Bess, I don't have a lot of time. I think Vlad kidnapped Amy."

"Of course the Impaler has her," Bess said, a little too loud.

"The dragon makes it obvious," Winnie said.

Bess turned on Winnie. "You're the one who first mentioned the dragon to me. Why?"

"I'm afraid I can't say. The police have asked me to keep certain things quiet. And Detective Howland was quite clear today."

"She saw something, didn't she?" Greg asked.

Bess looked at Greg and then slowly back to Winnie. "What's he talking about?"

It was Greg who answered. "The fourth body."

"Emily Baker," Bess said. "They found her right across the street, didn't they?" The details sprang to her mind in chunks. Greg pointed out the window toward the grassy lot flanked by two-story brick businesses on either side. There had once been a building there, an old family-owned hardware store—

the type of business driven to extinction in the age of the big box store; Bess remembered when they finally tore it down about ten years ago.

"It's true," Winnie said. "I called the police. I was coming to open up the society. But they kept most of it out of the papers, including the graffiti on the building next to her head." She paused for the drama of it. "It said, 'Margaret Swallowed Whole. The Dragon's Revenge.'"

"Saint Margaret," Bess whispered.

"Exactly my first thought," Winnie said, nodding.

"Why would the police keep it out of the papers?" Bess asked.

"To weed out fake tips. If you know about the graffiti, then you'd have to have something to do with it," Greg answered.

"Detective Howland told me he didn't want reporters to find out I was the one who found the body because he knew they'd hound me for details I couldn't give," Winnie explained.

Greg quietly leaned in. "There's something I need to show you."

"So show it."

"Not here. It's at my house," Greg said.

"I am *not* going to your house."

"God damn it, Amy!" he yelled.

Bess jumped and choked back a gasp.

"I don't think you were invited," Winnie said carefully.

"I mean 'Bess,'" Greg sighed. "I'm sorry."

"What is it you want to show me?" Bess asked.

"Amy's journal. She has things in there. I think they might be clues to who abducted her."

Winnie squinted at her. "I don't know anything else. I'm forbidden to even be talking about this at all."

"So show it to the police," Bess said.

"The police didn't care," Greg said, his voice louder now.

"I have to admit, I wasn't too impressed with our police force," Winnie said. "And I'd rather keep to myself as much as possible. I like my privacy."

"Oh well then!" Bess said. "I'm not a fucking detective. This isn't a Hardy Boys mystery and I'm not looking for clues." She thought back to Detective Howland and added, "They don't need the Scooby Gang running around town trying to catch a villain."

"But you *are* looking for clues, aren't you?" Winnie asked. "It's why you're here."

"Did the police care about what you told them?" Greg asked.

"Who says I told the police anything? What would I even tell them?" Bess answered.

"Look. Winnie here knows where you're going. You're safe. Greg Leeds. Three e's. The house is over on Aviary Street, by the river."

Bess's eyes lit up. "The river?"

"Yeah," Greg replied. "Reddington River?"

"Sounds a lot like Bevington," Bess mumbled.

"I guess. If you've been drinking."

"What about Bevington?" Winnie asked. The sharp older woman seemed wholly confused and Bess felt sorry for bringing Greg here.

"Okay, I'll go," Bess said.

Winnie waved her off and headed toward the back of the building, obviously finished with Bess altogether.

"You can follow me in your car. There's a public parking lot about a block down the street," Greg said. For a moment Bess considered that maybe he was lying, maybe he didn't live there, maybe it was all a trick. But the lure of more clues was too much for her.

"Do you have a basement, Greg?" Bess asked.

"By the river? Hell no, it would flood."

Greg's home was a tiny grey Craftsman with a little concrete porch and red shutters. The front door opened into a tiny living room area on the right and a dining room and kitchen on the left. Bess let Greg enter first and remained close to the door as he walked toward a worn, navy blue couch.

"Do you want to sit down?" he asked.

"No. Just show me the journal."

"I could get you a drink? I have Fat Tire, you like that, right?"

Bess's hand snaked into her jeans pocket, fingers curling around the pepper spray. "I want to know what I'm doing here."

"Okay, now, here's the thing," Greg said, grinning. "Now don't be angry with me, Bess. Promise me you won't be angry with me?"

The steady thump of Bess's heart picked up. "There's no journal, is there?"

"Aw, now, Bess. You guessed. I was going to do a big reveal and you ruined it." Greg was still smiling at her, his voice light, as if he was building up to a great punch line.

ANTIOCH

"I'm leaving," Bess said. Her brain was setting off all the internal alarms. Her vision tunneled as she stepped back toward the door.

"No!" Greg barked. "Now Bess, I needed to hear what's going on with you. But not there. Not with the old woman hanging around. Tell me what you know. Tell me what you told the police." He moved toward her.

"Amy's been contacting me. Through my radio. The one I showed you."

"Fuck," Greg muttered.

"I don't know how she sends them."

"You know if they find me, you're caught."

"What's that supposed to mean?"

There was a sudden bang that made Bess jump and cry out. She turned to Greg, at first thinking he must have hit something, then realized he hadn't made the sound at all. It had come from below them. Somewhere around the middle of the living room floor, something was knocking, rustling.

"I thought you didn't have a basement," Bess said.

"I don't. It's raccoons in the crawlspace. They get down there and tear shit apart."

"*Amy?*" Bess screamed the name as loud as she could.

"What the fuck, Bess? What the fuck are you doing?"

"*Amy!* I'm here, Amy!"

The rustling below them quieted. Bess tried to run forward into the house, but Greg grabbed her around the waist and slung her easily back toward the door. "You couldn't wait to run out of here a second ago, now you're trying to get in," he said, laughing.

"She's here, isn't she?"

"I don't know what you're talking about, Bess." He grabbed her wrist. "So which is it? In or out? Because I think we should really talk some things out."

"Let me go."

"Are you sure?" Greg leaned down, his face only inches from hers.

"Fuck off, Greg."

Bess pulled the pepper spray from her jeans pocket. She closed her eyes tight and held her breath as she sprayed blindly toward Greg's face. As soon as his grip on her wrist loosened she turned and fled from the house. Her eyes were still closed and she tripped immediately on the steps and fell, her knees hitting the ground hard. The breath she'd been holding whooshed out of her in a sharp wail of pain. Forcing herself to ignore the throbbing in her knees, she pushed up to her feet and ran down the street as fast as her legs would take her.

She heard someone behind her, a man shouting her name. She still had the pepper spray held tight in her hand. The man was gaining on her, she felt him behind her, close enough to touch her. Summoning all her courage, she glanced back over her shoulder.

Detective Howland was on her heels. The sight of him startled her so much she tripped again. The pepper spray shot across the street as her fingers spread and she tried to catch herself. Detective Howland rammed into her, whether on purpose or accident Bess couldn't tell. Her cheek mashed into the loose grit of the sidewalk and Howland's weight pressed the air out of her body.

Within seconds he was off of her, but Bess

couldn't move. Her lungs were burning, her muscles were jelly.

"Are you okay?" the detective asked. He was on his knees next to her, gingerly brushing her hair back from her face.

"He's got Amy," Bess gasped. "He has her in the basement."

"Shhhh, you're okay. Don't try to talk. Can you sit up?"

Bess sat up slowly and turned her head away from him, trying to hide the tears that flowed down her soft brown cheeks. "Where did you come from?"

"Winnie Tate called me after you left the historical society. She was worried. Said you said something about the river." He was huffing lightly, out of breath.

Bess scampered over and retrieved her pepper spray. "I was with a man named Greg Leeds. He lives right down the street. He's Amy Eckhardt's boyfriend."

"Really?" he said, stunned. "I wasn't aware Amy Eckhardt had a boyfriend."

"How could you not know that?" Bess asked.

"Well, how do you know this man?" he asked, avoiding the question.

"We . . . dated."

"Are you serious?"

"Yes," she said, suddenly feeling defensive. She stood up and brushed herself off, feeling momentarily superior until Detective Howland also stood up and towered over her. "It was one date." Her cheeks were burning.

"You don't have to explain yourself to me. I'm sorry. It's none of my business." He smiled at her. "Look, why don't I drive you home?"

"What about Greg Leeds?"

"We can talk more about it in the car. I'll radio it in, get someone down here."

"My car's right there," Bess told him, pointing to the parking lot where she'd left it. It was only a few feet away.

Howland looked at the lot and then back down the street. "Well do you want to talk in your car? I can call about Greg Leeds on my cell if you'd like. But we really do need to discuss some things."

"Don't you want to look for Amy?" Tears pricked the corners of her eyes.

"Let's talk first."

Bess allowed herself to be led toward her car. Detective Howland opened the driver's side door for her and she got in without a word. There had once been a few stores along Aviary—a tiny grocery, movie rentals, a small curio shop—but all these had been closed for decades now, only their hulled-out shells remained, a reminder of the way life used to be, when communities were closer and lives more connected.

As promised, Howland contacted dispatch and had cars sent to Greg's house. Bess didn't know the address, but she described it to Howland and he relayed it to the dispatcher. The two looked through the dash and out toward the river. It was calm and muddy like the rain-filled tread mark of a humongous pickup truck.

"So, what was all this about?" Howland asked. "Winnie Tate thought you were going to throw yourself into the river or something."

"Why would she think that?"

"You tell me. She said you were raving, not

72

making any sense. And I find you hysterical out there on the street. What were you running from, Bess?"

"Greg Leeds. He attacked me." Her voice was dull. All the feeling had drained from her, maybe from the adrenaline rush earlier.

Scott Howland sighed and pulled a pack of cigarettes out of the car console. "Do you mind if I smoke?"

"No, I don't mind."

"Would you like one?"

"No thanks, I quit."

"Yeah, me too."

"Do you know who Irene Bolam is?" Bess asked, her eyes far away.

"I don't believe I do."

"She was a banker in New York. She died in 1982."

"Well, that explains why I don't know her," he said, exhaling.

"Some people thought she was Amelia Earhart. They thought that she'd been found in a Japanese prison and repatriated back to the United States, but was given a new identity. There are some books about it."

"Is that what you think? That this banker was really Earhart?"

"Nope. I think Amelia Earhart died on a fucking island. But it's a neat idea, huh? A whole new life where you can watch and listen to people theorize about you. And only you would know." Bess blinked rapidly against the sunlight off the river. "You could take the biggest mistake of your life and forget it. Start fresh."

"She'd still know the truth."

"Sure, she'd know."

"Seems to me, all that knowing and never being able to tell, that'd be enough to drive someone crazy. It'd eat away at me."

"I guess it depends on how badly you want to forget. I think the Impaler kidnapped Amy Eckhardt. I believe it. And I want her to be okay." She fought back tears.

Detective Howland smiled at her. "Amelia Earhart sounds a lot like Amy Eckhardt, is that why you brought up the banker?" He took a final draw from his cigarette before flicking it out the window. "You need to know, we made an arrest in the Impaler case. It's what I wanted to tell you."

"What? Who is it?"

"Some guy named Tam Gillis. We've been building a case against him for months, finally got enough to charge him."

"And *he's* the guy?"

"Everyone gets a day in court. But between you and me, this guy's guilty. You should have seen his house. Full of Satanic symbols, it was enough to give you the creeps, I'll say that."

"And Amy?"

"No Amy, I'm afraid. I never thought the two were related."

"Why wouldn't they be related? This makes no sense. People don't disappear for no reason."

"Amy's the type of person that might disappear for no reason."

"What does that mean?" Bess asked.

"I know you've been on the case for a couple days now, but I've been on it a mite longer. Amy was a troubled young lady. I think it's more likely she started a new life as a banker than died on an island." He sounded so confident. Bess wanted to believe him, she wanted this to all be the truth. She imagined police officers in riot gear busting down Greg's door and walking a frightened—but *living*—Amy Eckhart out of his house. "I don't want to see you get hurt, Miss Jackson. And I'm very much afraid that's what'll happen if you keep poking around like this. You don't need to solve any crimes. It's all over."

"But what about Greg?" she asked. "You say you know all about Amy, but you didn't even know she had a boyfriend."

"To my knowledge, Amy wasn't seeing anyone. Where exactly did you hear otherwise?"

Bess paused. She didn't want to admit to calling Monica Bortles or incriminate herself for impersonating an officer. "Greg told me. He mentioned it today."

Detective Howland seemed to consider this for a moment. "Well, someone's probably at his house right now. We'll get to the bottom of it."

Bess followed Detective Howland to the police station to give a statement and file a report about Greg and then drove home in silence. She knew he was right. She couldn't keep poking her nose where it didn't belong and expect to come out of this unscathed. At the same time, she knew Amy was reaching out to her for help. The police said they caught Vlad and there was no sign of Amy. But sometimes the police made mistakes.

Her yard was devoid of decoration, dragon masks or otherwise, and she trudged up to the house without enthusiasm. She unlocked the door and deadbolt with different keys and absently wiped her feet on the doormat before walking into the cool dark interior of her house.

The room seemed the same as always, but with small, yet important, differences. The drawers of her desk were pulled out, the contents protruding ever so slightly over the edges. The things on top of her desk had been swept off the side and onto the carpet. Her couch cushions were in place, but had a fluffed look, as if they'd been taken up, plumped, and replaced. Bess grabbed a beer out of the refrigerator, opened it with her tulip opener, and walked back to her bedroom.

The door was open, which wasn't unusual. The bedsheets were crumpled on the floor—also not unusual. In fact, her room was normally in such a disarray she couldn't honestly say if anything was different. If the room were tidy it would have been a better giveaway.

She should have been afraid, she knew that, but her insides felt numb. Her nerves were desensitized from overuse. She checked her closets and under her furniture, making sure she was alone in the house.

Her mind slid to her radio and she began to chew her lip anxiously. Apparently she was not totally without feeling. She drank her beer and traipsed to the garage, saying a silent prayer that she wouldn't find the radio smashed on the concrete. Bess's notebook was sitting in its regular spot on the card table next to her wholly intact radio. She picked up the notebook and noticed with sadness, but no real surprise, that most of the pages had been ripped out. Only the front and back covers remained, with a few blank pages in between. All of her notes were gone.

"It's fine," she said to herself. "I don't need them."

The police had arrested the murderer. And if someone else was breaking into her house and stealing her notes, well, she would take comfort in the knowledge that it wasn't Vlad. Or maybe it was.

Bess didn't turn on the radio. She was a little afraid of it. Instead, she tried the local news. Detective Howland hadn't given her much information about Tam Gillis except that he'd been a Satan worshipper. And didn't that feel fine? Blaming all this chaos on the biggest, baddest evil man knew how to articulate, yeah, that felt just right. And then they could all go back to believing these sorts of things didn't normally happen. That this was some outlier event that could never touch them again.

As suspected, the news was full of juicy facts about Tam Gillis. Tam was a young nineteen-year-old loner, living near the center of town, working at Morning Glory Café only two blocks from his apartment. Police had suspected Gillis since he showed up at the funeral of the Impaler's second victim, Ashley Bunkirk. Others in attendance said they didn't recognize Gillis and that he was acting strange—lurking in the back of the crowd, not speaking to anyone. He was later seen hanging around the area of the park where Ashley's head had been found.

Police began watching him and picked up on some

odd behaviors. Several of his neighbors had called in noise complaints, claiming loud chants and wails could be heard through the walls at all hours of the night. When police arrived at his apartment to follow up on these complaints, officers noted not only unusual music coming from the residence, but also strange smells.

Bess wasn't clear on how the police had finally landed on Tam Gillis belonging to a Satanic cult. Several small things led to one big search warrant and then there they were, with a house full of pentagrams, knives, and what the news anchors described as "herbs common in the dark arts." Bess eyed her spice cabinet warily, wondering which of the contents might betray her.

Bess clicked off the television and sighed. If Detective Howland thought this was the guy, she would trust him, but she had her doubts. A little voice inside her head asked her exactly *why* she trusted the detective. Certainly the man had done nothing to earn any trust. He'd dismissed her entirely. But it was easier to trust the people who claimed to be in charge. At the end of the day, Bess wanted him to be right.

Her stomach growled. She glanced at the clock. It was too late to cook, but not too late to order Chinese. Within forty-five minutes, she was feasting on General Tso's chicken and fried dumplings. Her house had been put back into the same general semblance of order it'd held before and she was feeling mostly happy.

After stowing the leftovers safely in the fridge, Bess drew a hot bath and slid in, letting the water lap up around her chin as she sank low under a thin layer of bubbles. She let her mind drift. The past few days had put her brain into overdrive and it felt good to allow it to stop. To be quiet for at least a few minutes.

The dream was too long. It splashed into her mind like a salty wave, burning her cuts and scrapes in one screaming blast before lingering like a phantom. Her dream-self gasped into existence in the garage. Always the garage. The radio was on, the static a dissonant screech in her ears. She wanted to turn it off but she couldn't make herself move in that direction.

Something else was drawing her attention. A noise from the living room. A soft low beat, all bass and reverb. She moved like a cloud, her essence breaking up and reforming and pulling apart before coming back together. The door opened for her, but she could have passed right through.

The living room was darker than usual. Bess could barely see the shapes of her furniture. An overhead light that didn't exist outside of the dream suddenly clicked on. There was a knocking on the door. This time the knocks didn't frighten Bess. She eased calmly toward the door and reached for the handle.

"I wouldn't do that," a voice from behind her said. Glancing back, she saw Detective Howland. He stood in her kitchen holding a brown paper bag of popcorn. There were greasy splotches soaking through the paper. "They want you to go out."

"Who is it?" Bess asked.

"It's a mystery to everyone." He tossed a piece of popcorn into his mouth and crunched.

Bess peered through the window. There was someone there. She could see a shape, it was just outside her field of vision, but the blurred edges of a person were visible. She pressed herself closer, trying to see, but a sudden flash of lightning made her step back. Thunder rumbled through the house.

"They want in," Bess said.

"You're not wrong," Howland replied, grinning.

The knocks were deliberate and paced.

1 Mississippi . . . 2 Mississippi . . .

They started to move down the wall toward the window where Bess stood—just as they had the previous night. Bess stepped up to the glass, trying to get a view of the person. They were shorter than Bess anticipated, the dimensions not quite making sense, until she realized the head was missing. A thin woman's body, dressed in dirty red tights under an equally dirty black skirt and top. Bess stepped away as the figure approached the window, bleeding knuckles leaving burgundy clots on the glass with each knock.

"Is it Amy?" Bess asked.

"Could be. Could be one of the others." Howland chomped his popcorn like a horse and Bess turned to look at him again. He was closer now, next to her couch, and Bess went to him. She could feel heat coming off his body from three feet away. There was more thunder before the sky let loose and rain smacked against the roof.

"Why can't you find the bodies? If Gillis is the killer, where are all the bodies?"

ANTIOCH

"It's not important, Bess. These things never are. You're missing the point." He gestured toward the window. Lightning illuminated the headless woman, she shimmered in the rain. She used her blood to make squiggles and shapes on the glass. Slowly the crude spiraling coil of a dragon began to form and then bleed away under the torrent.

Detective Howland's hot breath puffed against her neck as he leaned down to whisper into her ear. "This could get messy."

Goosebumps raced down her neck and arms. He was so close that when she turned, her cheek brushed the soft worn fabric of his shirt. He laced his arms around her, hands closing at the small of her back, holding her there. Bess didn't struggle. Their faces were too close together, Bess couldn't make out his features anymore, only the angled plane of his stubbled cheek, a flash of white from his eyes. She pressed herself full against him, felt the hard lines of his body working into her own, fitting her like a puzzle piece. Her body throbbed with heat, she was dizzy with it.

"Is this what you were looking for?" he asked her, his mouth so close to hers.

"I was looking for Amy," she whispered, her hands snaking behind him, trying to pull him closer.

"But Amy's dead."

Bess was on her feet before she even knew where she was. Something had yanked her from her dreams. Her eyes swept around her bedroom, swiping at her cheeks with both hands, a phantom tingle prickled across her skin. There was a high-pitched ringing in her ears. Then she saw it, a brown spider about the size of a quarter scuttling across her pillow, looking for a dark place to hide.

"Fuck!" she cried and scanned the room for something to crush it with. Grabbing a black pump from beneath her bed she quickly mashed it down, leaving only a dark smear of guts and legs.

"I guess it's a good day to wash the sheets." She laughed as if it was funny.

The house was still and quiet as Bess loaded her spider-stained sheets into the washer. It was still early and she was at first grateful to the spider for waking her up so she wouldn't be late. Then she realized it was Monday. Bess didn't work on Mondays. She felt a renewed satisfaction that the spider was dead. Her mind swung back to the dream she'd had, but she could only remember fragments. Feelings. A sense that things were not as they should be.

Sunlight shone through the living room window and splashed across her face. Dark smudges across the glass broke apart the light, diffusing it, tinting it. The glass was caked in mud, bits of grass jutted out from the clods.

Without thinking she sprinted out the front door and into her yard, her bare feet squishing into the wet lawn. Enormous hunks of grass had been torn up and were now prominently featured against her siding, front door, and windows.

"Kids, yeah?" Bess's neighbor, Rebecca, was at her mailbox.

"I don't . . . Did they get your house too?" Bess asked, hating how much she needed Rebecca's house to also be wrecked.

"No, but they sure did a number on you. And in

the middle of that storm, too. I'll never understand teenagers." Rebecca smiled.

"I didn't even know it rained," Bess said, still staring at her house.

"Seriously? Girl, it was like a fucking monsoon or something. It woke me up around three."

"I slept through it."

"You must have been exhausted—knocked out. Here, some of your mail was mixed up in mine. Your paper was in my yard too."

Bess collected the small bundle from Rebecca. The front page of the paper caught her eye. "What the hell?"

"I know, can you believe it? Mayor Butler's crazy if he thinks he's going to get reelected after this one."

"This says it's Wednesday." Bess pointed to the date on the front of the paper.

Rebecca looked blankly at Bess. "So what?"

"So, it's Monday. Don't you think that's odd?"

"I think it's odd you think it's Monday on a Wednesday . . . "

"Wait, what time is it?"

"Oh gee, I guess it's about ten? Are you feeling okay? You don't look so good."

"What? Yeah, I'm fine. It's just . . . I don't know. I feel like I had a dream about this last night." She smiled at Rebecca to prove she was fine. "I could have sworn it was Monday." She glanced back down at the letter in her hand. It had her address penned on the front, but no return address and no stamp or postmark.

"Eh, don't worry about it. Well, if you're fine I've got to get back inside, there's a million things to get done."

JESSICA LEONARD

"Of course, you go on. Thanks for the mail."

Bess walked back inside, aware but not concerned about the soggy mud-prints she was leaving on the carpet. The clock in her kitchen said it was 8:24, as did the clock on her nightstand. The only problem being that they'd both said 8:24 before she'd gone outside too. She tapped the screen of her cell phone and was greeted with the harsh reality that it was in fact 10:17 on Wednesday. What had happened to Monday and Tuesday?

Deep enormous fear reached into Bess's chest and pulled at her insides. Her frantic mind tried to bring reason to the unreasonable. She was confused, she'd forgotten what day it was. It happened to people all the time, like Rebecca said. The days become too routine, they blend together, they lose distinction. Except her days had been anything but routine, and she couldn't shake the truth: She'd lost a full day.

"I have to go to work," she told herself, trying to calm down. Work was routine and routine would help. Routine would not steal her time.

Carol was front and center as Bess walked through the front door of The Rabbit Hole.

"I thought you were on vacation," she said.

"Oh, no. Sorry, I guess I wasn't very clear. Is it okay that I'm here?"

"Fine with me. I'm checking inventory, but we got a shipment in. You want to handle that?" Carol nodded toward the back of the store where a stack of boxes was nestled against the wall.

"Yeah, of course. Hey, did you hear about that arrest they made? With the murders?" Bess tried to sound casual.

"Well, I'm not a hermit living off the grid in the woods, so yeah, I heard." Carol didn't look up from her clipboard.

"Do you think he did it?" Bess asked.

"Considering he pretty much confessed, I'd say it's a good bet."

"Is that right? I hadn't heard he confessed."

"So you're the one living in the woods."

Bess waited for Carol to elaborate, but it was clear she was in no mood for chit-chat. Bess put her purse away and started to work on the shipment without another word. With something to keep her busy, Bess felt almost normal. The day passed like any other. There were no mysterious knocks, no lost time. By the end of the day, the idea of going back home didn't make her happy. That's where things went wrong.

Instead of collecting her purse, Bess walked to the bar and sat down on a stool across from Lucy.

"What do you want?" Lucy asked. Bess pretended it was a pleasant, *What can I get you?* instead of an annoyed, *Why are you here?*

"Can I get a beer? You know, if you aren't busy. I thought maybe we could talk."

"Am I getting fired?"

"Jesus fucking Christ, Lucy. This is why we don't talk."

"Sorry, shit. What do you want to talk about?" Lucy popped the cap off a Fat Tire without even asking and Bess briefly considered if she was too predictable before settling on being grateful for the drink.

"Carol was saying that guy confessed to all those murders. Did you hear about that?"

"You really want to hang out and talk about a murderer? *This* is why we don't talk."

Bess gulped her beer and hung her head, eyes on the bar. Carol's voice was in her head telling her this was what she got for not maintaining any real friendships. When she needed someone she was forced to socialize with a perky blonde she had nothing in common with.

"It wasn't even a confession anyway," Lucy said.

"What was it then?"

"The poor guy is getting bullied by the cops, that's what it is." Lucy pulled her iPad out from behind the counter and began tapping the screen ferociously. "Look at this video," she said, shoving the screen under Bess's nose.

The camera angle looked down on a Spartan room containing a table and a couple of chairs. On one side of the table Bess recognized Tam Gillis from the pictures she'd seen on the news. Detective Howland was on the opposite side and Bess felt a sudden flush as flashes from her dream reemerged.

"Where did this come from?" Bess asked.

"I don't know," Lucy huffed. "It's on fucking YouTube."

"But the police wouldn't release this, right?" Bess's mind searched back to every crime drama and made for tv documentary she'd ever seen and tried to recall if a confession was ever reported before a case went to trial.

"Do you want to see it or not?" Lucy asked.

"I do, yeah." She suppressed the urge to apologize.

Lucy pressed play and the low-resolution black and white video began.

ANTIOCH

A few seconds ticked by before Detective Howland finally spoke. "Do you know Ashley Bunkirk?"

"No. She was just a lady that came into the shop," Tam replied. His voice was softer than Bess expected, like a little boy.

"So you did know her?"

"I took her order sometimes. She was a nice lady. She was nice to me."

"Why were you at her funeral?"

"She was nice to me. I was sorry she died."

There was a long pause while Detective Howland shuffled some papers around in front of him. The camera blinked. A quick cut. The two men were seated in the same chairs, but now Tam was leaned over the table, his forehead pressed against the edge, his hands dangling down between his legs.

Detective Howland again spoke first. "So let's go over your dream again. What happened to Ashley?"

"Um . . . she was unconscious? And then I would have stabbed her. Then used the branch cutter to . . . " Tam sat up and wrapped his arms around his stomach. "I don't like this."

"No one likes it, Tam, but it's important. If I'm going to be able to help you at all, we need to get through it."

"The branch cutter was to cut off her head." Tam snuffled lightly and Bess wondered if he was crying.

"And it had a serrated edge, right, Tam?"

"It did," Tam said quietly.

At this point the recording ended.

"Seems like a confession to me," Bess said, looking into her drink. She didn't believe her own words, but she wanted to hear what Lucy thought. She wanted to hear the conspiracies come from someone else's mouth.

"Are you kidding? What was that break in the middle? We have no idea how much time lapsed there. And didn't you hear the cop ask him about a dream? What the fuck is that about? I don't trust it." Lucy's voice had been rising steadily as she spoke, and the last couple lines came out like shrill squeaks. Suddenly self-conscious, she glanced around to make sure there weren't any customers within earshot.

"I don't think I've ever heard you so riled up, Lucy."

"Well, like you said, we don't talk. You don't know me at all." Lucy had tucked her iPad back out of sight and was swiping absently at the counter with a rag— her usual "look busy" routine.

"That's true." Bess felt a twinge of guilt that she quickly pushed down. Lucy didn't need to like her. She needed to respect her. But still, it was nice to have someone to talk to. "So, who are you? Tell me what you think," Bess said.

"It doesn't feel right. I think they wore him down in there until he gave up. And even then it doesn't feel like a confession. I'm not sure what happened, not exactly. But I don't think he did it."

"A confession like that, it wouldn't be admissible in court. There's no way a judge would allow that."

"Maybe that's why it was leaked. It's worthless in court, but it can sway public opinion, or maybe persuade someone to come out with real evidence."

Bess examined her drink and considered. "If I'm being honest, I hope he is the Impaler. I'd sleep better knowing the Impaler was locked up."

ANTIOCH

"Yeah, but remember, as long as they have this guy, they aren't looking for anyone else," Lucy said.

They aren't looking for Amy.

Bess finished her drink in one long swallow. "I should go home. I don't know what I'm doing here, anyway."

Lucy's eyes went wide at the abrupt shift but only waved halfheartedly in the direction of Bess's already turned back.

Bess jogged to her car and checked the backseat before getting in and quickly locked the door behind her. The world didn't feel any safer today.

Her home didn't look different when she came in and, unlike the feeling of walking to her car, she took this familiarity as a sign that things were okay. She would take any assurance she could get. On the counter, Bess noticed the plain white envelope Rebecca had given her that morning along with her paper. Part of her wanted to toss it unopened into the trash. That part was quickly overruled by her curiosity, which would never allow such a thing.

With one slender finger she wiggled the flap open and pulled a single white sheet of paper from the envelope. Across the center of the paper Bess saw two short sentences scrawled in a hurried but elegant cursive.

Tam is innocent. Dragon still loose.

6

SOMEWHERE NEAR THE river there is a house with a basement. And sometimes when it rains too much, like it has been lately, that basement begins to flood. A pump exists to drain the water, but negligence, or a different sort of purposefulness, has kept it off most of the time. Besides, there's nothing too important in there. Nothing that could ruin.

If you were to drive by the house you wouldn't notice it at all, sandwiched between two identical white concrete slab homes. There's some debris in the yard and the grass next the house is in desperate need of a weed eater, but all these small imperfections make it blend in rather than stand out. The lot is small and the backyard is surrounded by a rundown wooden privacy fence that was probably once a golden brown, but is now mostly grey. The "Beware of Dog" sign on the gate hangs askew.

Today you are walking by on the cracked sidewalk. There are dandelions poking up through the cement and you avoid stepping on them. The same way you avoid broken glass and dog shit. Your eyes are mostly down, but outside of this particular house, you happen to look up. A woman stands in the front window, her somber face a soft shadow in the bright sun. You wave, but don't really notice when she doesn't wave back. It was more an empty gesture on your part, anyway.

At night the lights go on like any other home. Light glows through the lone basement window, long and thin at the back of the house, but it's obscured by the fence. Shadows pass by the windows. Unrecognizable shapes that bend and move unnaturally behind the folds of sheer curtains.

You go into the house at night. Maybe you're looking for something. Maybe you heard a noise. Maybe you just needed to be there. Maybe this house called to you. The inside is mostly empty, but clean. Like someone's recently moved in. You see boxes stacked on the couch and a broom leaning against the dining room wall—the only decoration. The kitchen is pristine. You'd bet a meal's never been cooked on the stove. You check the fridge and find it empty. From the back of the house you can hear sounds, like scraping. There is a door at the end of the hall and you see light glowing from underneath it.

You move quietly along the soft grey carpet, keeping to the sides of the hall to avoid squeaky floorboards because you saw that on TV one time. Or maybe you read it in a book. Walk on the sides of the steps to avoid creaks. As you approach the door you smell something rancid and pull the collar of your shirt up over your nose and mouth.

JESSICA LEONARD

The door opens before you reach it. You duck into a dark bathroom. A man runs out of the room at the end of the hall. You lean back into the shadows. Try to make yourself smaller—less noticeable. He jets past the bathroom. His footsteps ring hollow through the house. You hear the front door open before banging shut. His features were impossible to make out in the dark. But the man is tall.

You emerge from your hiding spot and head straight for the room at the end of the hall. The smell has intensified so you breathe through your mouth, only then you can sort of taste it. You gag a little and feel the bile rising up into your throat, but you choke it back down with effort.

At first, you can't tell where the smell is coming from, but the ominous cloud of flies massing around the closet clues you in. The rest of the room contains a small desk and chair, a bookshelf, and a mini fridge. The bookshelf has four narrow shelves all packed with thick hardback volumes. Looking through the titles, they seem to center on Christianity, its history and theory. On top is a decorative stone dragon statue, about a foot tall, with green and gold paint.

There is a notebook on the desk filled with drawings and doodles. You don't understand the notes, they appear to be written in a different language. You don't notice a pen or pencil and wonder if the man took it with him when he left.

You're sweating now, and whether it is from the heat of the room or the nausea from the smell you are not sure. But you know you have to get out soon. The closet is slightly ajar and when you go toward it the flies part like a curtain.

ANTIOCH

It's dark inside the room and darker still inside the closet. The white from the PVC pipes is obvious, but their length is interrupted every so often by dark blotches that your brain has trouble recognizing. It's too unfamiliar. It's too unexpected. Then slowly you're able to sort it all out and understand what you're seeing. Rotting body parts skewered like at a barbeque. The flesh is in various stages of decay, some of it moist and waxy, other parts dripping and dark. Tendons hang onto bone hang onto muscle as they stretch toward the floor. Liquified meat puddles and coagulates.

You back out of the room, unable to look away from the horror of the closet but also unable to stop yourself from fleeing. In your escape you pass right by the small, inconspicuous basement door. If there is anyone or anything down there you may never know. And that suits you just fine.

7

BESS HADN'T TURNED on her radio in days, but she knew eventually she would. It was two in the morning and she was no closer to sleep than she'd been at ten. Her brain wouldn't quiet. The nerves vibrated with anxious energy. Her options were to sit up all night or try calming herself with the radio. It seemed like an easy decision, but there was also a chance the radio would wind her up even more, sending her undesired communications.

She decided the risk was worth it. Wrapped in a long white terrycloth robe, Bess shuffled into the garage and switched on her radio. She slid between channels listening to a mix of piano, garbled talk, CB conversations, and traffic updates. The anxiety inside her slowly began to unspool. Exhaustion filled her limbs as tension ebbed away. Within minutes she was fighting to keep her eyes open and wondering why she never moved a futon out into the garage for nights like this.

Radio static followed her back into the house. She

94

left the door open and trudged toward the couch to lie down. Her eyes slid to the mud-spattered window, but only for a moment. It would have to be cleaned, but that could wait. Everything could wait.

When they were children, Amelia Earhart and her sister Muriel invented a game called Bogie, which involved creating elaborate maps of a make-believe world. They would explore their world and all of its wonders, monsters, and dangers. Years later, in her autobiography, Earhart wrote, "I know I can never be so terrified by anything met with in the real world as by the shadowy play creatures which lurked in the dark corners of the hay mow to attack us, or crept up the creaking steps from the lower stalls."

Her phone was ringing and for a brief, frantic moment Bess feared she'd overslept. But the clock said it was only 6 a.m., and Bess was filled with a whole new sort of fear.

"Hello?"

A deep, distorted, almost electronic voiced answered her. "The Dragon is still loose. Tam is innocent."

"Who is this?" Bess asked. Bile crept up her throat and she swallowed hard against it. A shiver slithered through her body.

"The Dragon is religious or has extensive knowledge of Christianity," the voice continued.

"Hi, I'm pretty sure the cops have their own tip lines for this sort of thing. Maybe you have the wrong number." The panicked edge in her voice betrayed her.

"Tam Gillis is innocent."

The line died and Bess set the phone on the

counter. The thread holding her together stretched a little more. She'd never asked for this. There was a steady weight pressing down on her chest, she felt off-balance, like she might fall over at any moment. Her breath was shallow. The bed was calling her name. Rather than lie back down and miss work, Bess showered and went in early.

The Rabbit Hole didn't open until nine, and in the thin quiet hours of the morning it was easier to accomplish paperwork. Spreadsheets were less daunting. Her mind didn't have time to worry about murderers and mysterious phone calls.

At five till nine she made her way through the darkened store to unlock the doors. She could see someone outside, waiting for them to open. She considered hiding in the back. When people were too eager for them to open, she resented it. Which probably wasn't the best business tactic, but it was a fact. More realistically, she decided to wait the five minutes until Wayne arrived for his shift. Wayne was never late, but he was never early either. He would come in through the back door at nine on the dot, ready to work, smile already in place.

Bess ducked back into a row of science fiction and pretended to straighten the books, her back resolutely to the entrance.

Like clockwork she heard Wayne's voice call out to the room, "Hey boss! You in here? It's going to be another beautiful day!"

"I'm here, Wayne!" she called back, waving a hand to signal her location. "We've got customers already, so I decided to wait for you."

"Always a good bet," he replied, not really listening.

ANTIOCH

Wayne flicked on the lights as Bess swung the door open expectantly, but the person who'd been out there was gone.

"I thought you said we had people," Wayne said.

"We did. Damn. I guess I pissed them off by not opening up earlier."

Wayne shrugged and ducked behind the counter to get his station ready for the day. Bess brewed a pot of coffee and poured two identical paper cups.

"You still take yours black?" Bess asked, handing Wayne a cup.

"Of course. You still take yours khaki?"

"I'd say it's more like caramel."

"Beige."

"Okay. It's beige."

"Just us this morning?"

"Yeah, but I think we can manage," Bess replied, motioning to the empty store.

"It'll pick up." Wayne sipped his coffee and winced against the heat. "Say, did you catch the news this morning?"

"I did not," Bess said, a sinking feeling in her stomach. "Please tell me it's something good."

"I guess that depends on who you are. But I saw that guy they arrested lawyered up. They're saying that leaked confession was coerced."

Bess laughed in spite of herself. "Coerced? Damned if that isn't a million-dollar word."

"Laugh if you want, but that's the word they used on the news." Wayne's gaze met level with Bess's but the usual fun was suddenly missing.

"Wayne, I wasn't making fun of you. It's just . . . such a lawyer word."

"Well, I'd imagine that's who told the man to say it," Wayne said, indignant.

"You're probably right. Who's the lawyer?"

"I've got no idea. Supposedly some big shot guy from out of town," Wayne said.

"The fuck would a big-time lawyer be doing representing a kid who worked in a coffee shop?" Bess was pacing back and forth with her coffee.

"Well, what I've heard is that this kid has some kinda high class family here in town. Somebody with deep pockets maybe." Wayne was grinning now, the gossip getting the better of him.

"I guess that could be. Rich folks in Antioch aren't unheard of." Bess looked at Wayne for a long time, studying his face. "What do you think? Do you think this kid is a killer?"

"Shit. I don't know. Lucy was going on and on at me yesterday about how the confession didn't feel right. And now I'm hearing it's a fake." He shrugged. "Would I be surprised if the police locked up the wrong guy to shut everybody up about a killer on the loose? No, I would not. Not even a small little bit. On the other hand, would I be surprised that some young white guy was torturing and killing women? Well, the answer to that is also no. For now, I don't trust nobody. My Facebook is swarming with people saying the devil possessed him."

"I've seen people blaming everything from Satan to Tom Hanks. I think you've got it right: trust nobody. That's a smart motto. I'm with you on that one. Also, since when did Lucy start caring about this sort of thing? She find social justice on Pinterest?"

Wayne laughed, a loud blurting sound, like it had

caught him off guard. "You be nice to little Lucy. She's a sweet girl. She's just figuring things out, and I'm proud of her."

"Wayne, you're proud of everyone. That's your thing."

"And you're cynical about everyone. That's *your* thing. At least my thing makes people happy." He sipped his coffee and gave her a superior little side-eye.

"You're right again, Wayne. You're on a roll today," Bess said.

She carried her coffee over to the bar and leaned against it, her lower back resting snug against the cold countertop. Wayne was right about her being cynical. She slid her phone out of her pocket. flicked through her most recent calls. and tapped the redial button.

"Hi," she said. "My name is Bess Jackson and I'd like to speak with Detective Howland. No message, just, please have him call me when he can. Thank you."

She ended the call and slid the phone into her pocket. The ball was in his court now. If the police were interested in the notes and phone calls, then they could act. Howland told her himself she shouldn't get involved.

It was nearly two before he called her back.

"What can I help you with today, Miss Jackson?" he asked. Bess waited a moment to see if he would add more, but he didn't.

"I'm sorry to bother you, I know you're busy." Ever polite.

"Actually, if it hadn't been you, I wouldn't have returned the call at all."

"What makes me special?" She hated herself for sounding like a flirt, and for wanting to flirt.

"I was afraid that if I didn't call you back I'd find you out in vigilante mode again." He sounded playful, less harsh than his original greeting.

"Nothing like that, Detective." She felt comfortable. They were friends chatting. She dove right in. "It's just, I've received a sort of ominous phone call and a note shoved in my mailbox, both saying that the killer is still on the loose. I thought you might want to look into it."

There was a long pause. Bess thought she could hear him rubbing his temples.

"Miss Jackson, why would someone contact you about any of this?" His voice was slow and deliberate, no longer playing.

"I don't know."

"Is it maybe because you've already inserted yourself into this case?"

"I never meant to. I never wanted any of that. Detective—"

"You should call me Scott. Don't you think it's time to dispense with these formalities?"

"I do not, Detective Howland."

"Suit yourself."

"I thought it was something I should report. Was I wrong?" Bess struggled to keep her voice calm, to keep the waver out. She picked up her coffee and sipped it carefully. Finding it cool enough, she gulped it.

"Yes. You were wrong. Look, we got our guy. He confessed. The department isn't looking for any new leads on a closed case, do you understand?" His voice rose ever so slightly.

"And what if you have the wrong guy?" Bess's heart hammered in her throat.

"Didn't happen. Have a good day."

The line went dead. Bess swiped one clammy hand against her slacks and took a few deep breaths to calm herself. The call hadn't made her feel especially comforted. If there was a killer out there, he might reasonably come after the woman poking around, trying to get the case reopened and the police back on the hunt.

"You look like you saw a ghost," Wayne said, coming toward her.

"I don't feel very good, that's all."

"Who were you talking to?"

"The police."

"Hm. Yeah, I'd say that's enough to make a person feel under the weather." He chuckled a little, but his eyes remained serious, searching her face. "What's happening, Bess? Why do you need the police? You don't seem yourself lately."

"Lately?" Bess let out a shrill sort of laugh that made Wayne jump. "Lately, you say? Wayne, I've not been myself for a long time. Shit. I don't even know what 'myself' feels like at this point. God damn. Things weren't right even before I started hearing things."

"Hearing things?"

"What would you do? If you thought the guy in jail was innocent, but the cops didn't care. What would you do? Because I don't have a clue."

"I wouldn't do a thing. It's not my place. Look, I'm real sorry if they've got the wrong person, but I've got to take care of my own. I'm not about to put my family in danger for some kid I never met."

"What kind of danger?" Bess asked.

"Unwanted attention is always dangerous, Bess. And what you're talking about draws attention. Is that what you called the police for? To tell them they have the wrong person?"

She nodded.

"I don't like it. Too risky."

Keeping her head down was so much a part of daily life that Bess no longer gave it much thought. She wondered what Amelia Earhart would do. Earhart the supposed government spy would probably stay quiet. But Earhart the gutsy aviator would probably spend her final breaths trying to tell the world the truth.

"Say, you know they still have that young adult Bible study at First Baptist. It's twice a week. You should go, you'd make friends," Wayne said.

"Thanks, but I'm good. You've got this, right?" she asked him. "I need to head to the back for a bit. You can holler if you need me."

He nodded and Bess tried to ignore the concern all over his face as she made her way back to the employee bathroom.

The bathroom was tucked behind the breakroom. It was unisex and single occupancy, with a lock on the inside of the door. Back when it had been Bess's job to clean the bathroom, she'd cursed Carol every day for her choice of all white fixtures, floors, and walls. The room looked like a nightmare sanitarium. A single light hummed and sputtered overhead.

Bess ran cool water from the sink over her hands, watching it spill down the drain. She turned off the water and studied her reflection in the mirror. Her brown eyes were tired and red. Her long dark elegant limbs juxtaposed brilliantly against the harsh blunt bathroom. She was an oasis of grace within a blatant and glaring backdrop.

There was a knock outside the door.

"Just a second," she called.

The knocking stopped.

Bess dried her hands and turned to the door and the gentle rapping resumed. Rolling her eyes, she reached for the deadbolt.

"Impatient asshole," she muttered just as the person on the other side slammed against the door, causing her to yelp and jump back a step. "What the fuck?"

The thin wooden door rattled against the frame as the stranger threw their weight at it.

Bess pressed herself against the far wall looking at the door in horror. She fumbled in her pocket for her cell phone and quickly dialed out.

"Thank you for jumping down The Rabbit Hole. This is Wayne, can I help you?" Wayne had created the greeting himself. No one made him say that.

"Wayne! It's Bess. There's someone outside the bathroom banging into the door like a psycho. I don't know what to do."

"Okay, no worries. Let me handle it." He hung up the phone and Bess closed her eyes, trying to hide in the darkness.

The banging stopped.

Bess kept her eyes closed, waiting for Wayne to give her the all clear. The voice she heard didn't come from outside the door. It was in there with her, next to her, so close she could feel the breath against her neck.

A furtive whisper: *"You were supposed to save me."*

The room felt colder. Bess kept her eyes squeezed tight against the presence next to her.

"He'll come for you next."

A sharp bang against the bathroom door caused Bess to yelp, her eyes flying open. Wayne was there, a sheepish look on his face.

"I didn't see anyone. When you didn't answer me I got a little panicked." He nodded back to the slim brass bolt that had once held the door closed and now was framed in splinters, its holster torn from the door frame.

"Oh god, Wayne, I've never been so happy for something in this store to be broken." She ran to him, flinging her arms around his neck.

"What got you so worked up?" Wayne asked.

"You didn't see anybody?" she asked in return.

"No, ma'am, not a soul. You know, we should probably tell Carol a customer broke the lock."

Bess laughed in spite of herself. "Oh god damn, Wayne. I'll say I broke it myself. That lock is the least of my worries."

They checked the store together, searching for anyone hiding among the shelves or under a counter. Bess secretly hoped to find a rabid raccoon tearing into the drywall, but had no such luck. Once they were both satisfied they were alone, Wayne retrieved the small tool kit Carol kept in the break room and hurried off to see if he could fix the bathroom lock.

Bess couldn't stop thinking about Tam Gillis and his supposedly false confession. If a killer was still out there, he'd know no one was looking for him. Now would be the time to take risks, to let his guard down. He would be at his most dangerous, but also most vulnerable. Bess decided to spend some time on her radio. Amy might be able to get a message out while Vlad wasn't looking.

Wayne returned to the front of the store looking proud of himself.

"You get it fixed?" Bess asked.

"Sure did. Doesn't look good as new. Not exactly. But it'll lock." The smile faded from his face and was replaced by one of concern. "You know what, Bess? I'm worried maybe you're wound a little too tight about this whole Impaler thing."

"You think I imagined someone banging against the bathroom door." It wasn't a question.

"I don't know. But there wasn't anyone here."

"I'm not an irrational person, Wayne. I won't let you paint me as one." Bess's voice rose slightly and Wayne put up his hands as if to shield himself.

"You aren't. I know, I know. But I think maybe you're getting, well, you know . . . "

"Too emotional?"

"No. Just upset. Naturally upset. We're all upset. It affects some people different, that's all." Wayne's eyes were kind and pitying. Bess struggled to stay calm, reminding herself that he was a good man. That he wanted to help her.

"I'm not crazy. But yeah, it is on my mind a lot. I wish I knew for sure if that guy they arrested was innocent. I wish I could talk to him."

"Well, then do it. If that will make you feel better, I say talk to the man."

"What do you mean?"

"He's not in Siberia, just jail. And last time I checked, prisoners were allowed to have visitors."

8

THE HOUSE WAS still and dark. Bess didn't turn on any lights, instead letting her eyes adjust and maneuvering through the hallway with the sort of efficiency that comes from years of repetition. She changed out of her work clothes and into black sweats and a plain white tee shirt. She was on a mission. It was only five o'clock and she had all night.

Once in the garage she flicked on an overhead light, wincing against the harsh burn. The radio had become an ominous presence all its own. It loomed, dark and daunting on the shabby card table, beckoning her to come to it. Once her sanctuary, now desecrated.

She tuned the radio to low static and waited for something to find her.

It started as a mumble. A distinct and even sound with the cadence and monotone of a newscaster. A distant hollow voice came through the radio:

ANTIOCH

Act One. Margaret of Antioch spurns the advances of Olybrius.

Act Two. Margaret of Antioch is tortured.

Act Three. Margaret of Antioch is swallowed by a dragon.

Act Four. Saint Margaret of Antioch is disgorged by the dragon.

Act Five. Saint Margaret of Antioch is beheaded.

The transmission began again, the same words like a recording on an eternal loop.

Act Three. Margaret of Antioch is swallowed by a dragon.

Act Four. Saint Margaret of Antioch is disgorged by the dragon.

Bess opened her notebook to a clean sheet and jotted down the five high points of Margaret's life. She was tortured and killed by Olybrius, but it was the Dragon who wanted revenge. Olybrius had his victory, he saw her decapitated. But the Dragon was made a fool of that day.

Act Six. The Dragon will have vengeance.

JESSICA LEONARD

She blinked at the variation in the message. "But who's the Dragon?" she asked aloud.

Act One. Margaret of Antioch spurns the advances of Olybrius.

A frustrated sigh escaped her lips. She stood up and stretched her arms above her head, closing her eyes. The transmission hummed.

Act Five. We have reached Act Five. Saint Margaret SAINT NOW SHE IS A SAINT is beheaded.

ACT SIX. The Dragon will have vengeance. The Dragon was not beheaded. The Dragon lives.

SEVEN DEAD WOMEN. SEVEN. We now have SEVEN.

"So does that mean Amy's already dead?" Bess asked the room. She now assumed she could be heard. She assumed that if she turned off the radio the voice would still drone on in the room, coming straight from the walls. She did not assume she could trust the voice. "Who is the Dragon? If it's not Tam Gillis, if he swallowed a saint once, then who the fuck is he?" she yelled into the empty space around her.

The radio went silent.

Then softly, the voice of a woman, tinged with that metallic ring of fear and exhaustion. Amy Eckhart.

108

He's the Devil.

Cold washed over Bess and she shuddered. The radio was still on, but there was no longer any sound. Bess reached forward and turned it off, yanking her hand back as if it shocked her, or for fear that it would.

Her mouth was dry and she had a sudden intense need for water. She backed out of the garage, not wanting to turn away from the radio even for a second. Once the garage door was closed she turned and immediately saw something on the front window, besides the lingering smears of mud. A white piece of paper was plastered to the glass and Bess could see ink bleeding through from the other side.

Her neighbor, Rebecca, was also out in the yard squinting at the paper. Bess slipped on a pair of black flats and rushed out.

"Hey," she called to her neighbor.

"Hey, Bess," Rebecca replied. Her voice was far away and distracted. Her eyes never left the paper. "What's this about?"

The note read: *Tam Gillis is innocent. Ask him yourself.*

"I don't know. I just . . . saw it. Did you see who left it?"

"No. Isn't Tam Gillis the Impaler killer?"

"Uh, you know, I'm not sure. I don't really—"

"It is," Rebecca answered her own question with a frank surety that was startling. "It definitely fucking is. What's going on here?"

"Jesus, I don't know."

"Well, let me tell you something, Bess Jackson. I don't know what you're into with all this, but I've got kids next door. I don't need any weird-ass occult bullshit showing up around here. No way. We moved here because it was a nice quiet area."

Bess was stunned. She'd always considered Rebecca to be . . . not quite a friend, but something like that. Always friendly and warm. "Becky, I would never in a million years do anything to put your kids in danger. I promise you."

Rebecca sighed. "I know. I'm sorry. But I gotta look out for mine, you know what I mean?"

"I do."

"Are you into all this demon stuff? Like the Impaler killer?"

"No. I swear I'm not. I don't know any more about this than you do."

"Well, you know a little more than me. Because there aren't any crazy notes stuck to my window telling me to talk to murderers." Rebecca crossed her arms at Bess.

Bess shrugged and pulled down the paper. It was wet and left little bits of torn white paper stuck to the glass and Bess had to pinch at them to get them off. By the time she'd gotten it all cleaned up, Rebecca had gone back to her own house.

"Okay," Bess said. "I hear you. I'll go ask him myself."

Somewhere in the distance she heard a low rumble of thunder.

The jail in Antioch was comically small. A little larger than Bess remembered the one-room sheriff's office

ANTIOCH

on *The Andy Griffith Show* being, but not by a lot. News vans circled the building, forcing Bess to park a full three blocks away and walk over. Every fifteen feet she encountered another reporter looking into a camera and delivering almost identical statements:

"Tam Gillis, age nineteen, is the first suspect to be charged in the murders of six women here in Antioch."

"The so-called Vlad the Impaler murders have kept the sleepy town of Antioch awake for nearly two years."

"Gillis, believed to have ties to the occult, worked in a local coffee shop here in town."

For the first time, it occurred to Bess that it might be difficult to get in to see Tam Gillis. Anyone coming in or out of the jail would be questioned by the reporters. This seemed like exactly the sort of attention Wayne had warned her against.

There was a news crew setup at the steps of the jail and once Bess began climbing them she had their attention.

"Excuse me, ma'am?" A slim woman in a red blouse and black slacks rushed toward her with a microphone in hand. "Are you here to see Tam Gillis?"

"No, thank you," Bess called, not looking at the woman. She was inside before the woman in red could ask her any other questions.

When she asked to meet and speak with Tam Gillis, the officers didn't seem to know what to do, or where to put her. He'd had no visitors and even his lawyer only called on the phone. They waved a handheld metal detecting wand over her body, pausing at her belt and again at the underwire of her bra. A small but sturdy woman was called in to do a brief over-the-clothes pat down.

111

JESSICA LEONARD

Bess had seen plenty of television shows depicting people visiting inmates through glass, or in large common rooms containing metal furniture and barred windows. The light outside those windows was always a bleak sepia color that denoted a world devoid of sunlight and joy.

Eventually, Bess found herself in a little gray room with a small square wooden table and two metal folding chairs with sunflower cushions on the seats. It looked like the same room she'd seen on Lucy's iPad, the one where Tam had been interrogated and confessed.

A guard brought in Tam. He was a small man, fitting in nicely with the room itself, as if it were sized for him specifically. His wrists and ankles were cuffed, forcing him to shuffle as he walked. He had clear, ice blue eyes that stayed on Bess as he was helped into the chair furthest from the door. Bess checked the ceiling for the camera that had recorded the confession and found it immediately. It was large and tan, with a constant red light glowing from the front.

"If you need anything, I'm right outside," the guard told her. "But we have to keep the door locked."

"I understand," Bess said.

Once they were alone, Bess stared at Tam. She had no idea how to begin.

"Are you a reporter?" he asked her.

"No," she replied. "I'm no one," and the sound of it made her feel nauseous.

"Why're you here?"

"I wanted to ask . . . if you were guilty." It was the most honest answer she knew.

"Do you think that if I was, I'd tell you?" He leaned

112

ever so slightly forward with his elbows on his knees. His hands folded together as if in prayer.

"I don't know. But I still have to ask."

"Why do you have to ask?"

Bess considered this for a moment. "It's kind of a long story."

"Well, I didn't kill anybody."

"Then why did you confess?"

"I didn't."

"No, you did. I saw it myself. You did confess."

"You saw what they let you see. That cop." He paused, unsure of his words. "That cop kept saying he needed me to say things. Needed me to say stuff so he could help me. He . . . god damn. I don't know how to explain it. I don't even understand myself. But I swear, I never thought I was confessing to anything." For the first time his eyes slid away and Bess became uncomfortably aware of how young he was. He looked afraid. He smelled of it.

"So, if it's not you, then who is it?"

"That's what I want to find out! Fucking hell, there's nothing I can do in here and no one would listen to me even if I gave them the killer's home address." Sandy blond hair tumbled into his eyes as he spoke. He brushed it back awkwardly with his restrained hands, using them like a club to bat at the hairs.

Bess didn't know why she was here. This all suddenly seemed absurd. "Well, do you know anything? Can you help me at all?"

"Help you do what?"

"I don't know. Find out who the killer really is?"

He studied her face, his young mouth set firm. He was sizing her up. And whether it was to lie to her or trust her, Bess did not know. "I was trying to find him. That's why I was at the funerals," he said finally. "They're making a big deal because people saw me at the funerals, but that's because I was looking for *him*."

"Why get yourself involved in a murder investigation at all?"

"A lot of reasons. I don't know. I knew Ashley. She was . . . she was nice."

"Does that mean you wanted to fuck her?"

Tam blushed hard, his fair skin burning. "I didn't."

"You make 'didn't' sound an awful lot like 'did.'"

"I loved her," Tam said quietly. "She came into the café all the time and she was so beautiful but so nice too. I couldn't have hurt her. Not ever."

"The police said you were a Satan worshiper," Bess said, choosing to ignore his declaration.

"That's ridiculous."

"Why?"

"I don't even believe in the devil."

"So then what's all this stuff they said they found? Noises? Herbs? Whatever. Explain it."

"Why the fuck should I explain anything to you? I don't even know who you are. And I'm not supposed to be talking to anyone without my lawyer."

"I'm not a cop, you don't need a lawyer. My name's Bess. I want to help."

Tam sighed. He chewed at the chapped skin of his lower lip. "The music is just music," he said. "It's not the '80s, metal doesn't equal satanic. And yeah, I have some books. But it's real light stuff, nothing you can't get from Barnes and Noble. I like reading about the occult. But I don't believe it, let alone worship anything. I'm a god damned atheist."

Bess smiled a little. She could see it. A young kid rejecting god in all his forms, checking out his alternatives. Rebelling like the little nerd he clearly was, by reading books. "What do you know about the Dragon?"

Tam perked up. She'd said the magic words, the ones that seemed to make everyone in this town take notice. "You know something, too," he said, a sly grin spreading across his face.

"I know there's a dragon, and I know you ain't him. So if you know more than that, tell me. Help me get you out of here. Help me save Amy."

"You think Amy Eckhardt's still alive?"

"Well, they haven't found her head yet, so I'm keeping my fingers crossed."

"Okay. I have some notes. A profile, you know? On some traits he probably has, who it might be. My aunt has all that stuff now. Go talk to her. She can give you everything." His eyes were gleaming.

"And who is your aunt? Where do I find her?"

"At the historical society mostly, her name's Winnie Tate."

"I know Winnie! I've already met her. Why the hell didn't she tell me?" Bess realized her voice was rising and caught herself before she actually started to yell. She glanced back toward the door, thinking of the guard outside. She scolded herself for getting too emotional.

"Look, please go talk to Aunt Winnie. She can give you all my notes."

"Why do you trust me?"

"I don't have anyone else. Aunt Winnie believes me, but she's old. The cops want to solve this and pretend to be heroes. I heard the FBI wanted to take the case over and our good old APD has been holding them off for a year. They need this solved in order to keep outsiders away from Antioch. They're going to lock me up forever. They're going to put me in a hole in the ground and never let me out again. I need to trust someone."

"Tam, I hope I can help you."

Bess knocked on the door. A smiling guard appeared and let her out. "I hope he was real polite to you," he said as she passed by.

"Of course, a regular gentleman."

She walked as fast as she could without actually breaking into a run. Once outside she picked up the pace, making it a skip-jog sort of hybrid. The reporter from earlier was waiting for her on the sidewalk. Bess put her head down, kept her eyes on the pavement as she rushed back to where she'd left her car.

As she approached her Oldsmobile Bess slowed down. Someone was leaning against the driver side door. It was Detective Howland.

"Were you out here waiting for me?" she asked.

"Nope, just a happy coincidence." He smiled and waved the cigarette he was smoking at her. "Stopped here for a smoke. Although, I did hear a rumor that a beautiful young woman was here today visiting our young serial murderer."

"Is there a law against that?" she asked, crossing her arms over her chest.

"Not at all." He took a slow drag from his cigarette and exhaled back away from her. "I hope you haven't gotten the wrong idea about things, Miss Jackson. I don't dislike you. The opposite, in fact. I want you to be okay. I worry about you."

"I appreciate that, Detective. I never thought you didn't like me." She forced a smile.

"I asked you before, call me Scott. I'd say we know each other well enough at this point. Let's be Scott and Bess. How's that sound?" Bess could smell his cologne ever so slightly on the breeze, the same scent from when she'd first visited his office. Something clean and masculine, and the smell stirred something inside her.

"Okay, I appreciate that, Scott."

"Yeah, I like the way that sounds." He leaned against the side of her car, casually, but Bess couldn't help but notice he was blocking the door. "If I came across as a little gruff before, it's because Antioch doesn't get a lot of cases like this. None, actually. And the press is already calling us a bunch of bumpkins. This is national news. The whole country is looking at us thinking we can't catch a god damn killer in a town so small you'd think we'd be able to find the motherfucker by default or something. Find the one guy I don't personally know and it's probably him."

"But what if it's someone you *do* personally know?"

"Was that a joke?"

"Not really."

"Well, I didn't know Tam Gillis before I arrested the little fuck, so there ya go."

"And you're certain it's him?"

"Absolutely. And having civilians running around sticking their beautiful noses in where they don't belong, well, that's the sort of thing that can really mess up a case. The law's a tricky beast. There are all sorts of loopholes out there that can let a killer out on the street."

"Or put an innocent man in prison."

"I guess for the sake of the argument, yeah, that's true." He stepped toward Bess so that they were less than a foot apart. He was taller than her. If she looked straight ahead, she'd be staring directly into his neck. She saw the flash of his throat as he swallowed and felt a strong urge to reach out and touch it. "So, to set my mind at ease, Bess, would you mind telling me what you're doing visiting my murder suspect?"

She stared up into his eyes and lied, "I'm writing a book."

"Come again?"

"A book. You know, I work at the book shop here, and if I were to write and publish a true crime novel about this case it would be huge. We could sell it exclusively through the store."

His eyes said he knew she was lying, but also something else. That he was happy with the lies. "That sounds like a real smart plan."

"I thought so. I'm just full of real smart ideas, Scott." She smiled at him, feeling a warmth spread from her center out.

Scott leaned in and lightly squeezed her shoulder. "It was nice seeing you today, Bess." His breath was coming quicker and she hoped she was the one responsible.

She stretched up and grazed her mouth against the rough stubble of his cheek as she whispered, "It's always a pleasure."

He cleared his throat with a gruff little growl and stepped back. "Well, let's hope the next time is under more pleasant circumstances." He stamped out his cigarette and left the butt on the ground at her feet.

ANTIOCH

Bess wondered what it would taste like to kiss him as she watched him ambling slowly to the jail.

She stayed where she was for a few moments, reveling in the hormone-fueled electricity skittering through her. She didn't trust Scott Howland. But she couldn't stop herself from wanting to touch him every time he got close enough. It was moments like this that reminded her exactly how long she'd been single, and how different it felt when someone else touched her.

The historical society was only a five-minute drive from the jail. Nothing in Antioch was ever more than ten minutes away from any other point in Antioch. Bess parallel parked in front of the building and strode to the door.

No one was in sight when Bess walked in. She slid into the gift shop and thought about all the magnets she could potentially steal in this unattended store. Maybe even several keychains. In the future, this shop would probably carry dragon keychains and little plastic snow globes that rained red down upon the town.

Heading back out of the little shop, Bess caught sight of Winnie sitting in the replica old-fashioned living room with a cup of tea and a book.

"You have a lot of spare time around this place I guess," Bess said.

Winnie jumped slightly but a smile immediately brightened her face. "We don't get many visitors, it's true."

"I assume you know why I'm here?"

"I wouldn't have the slightest idea." Winnie's smile didn't waiver. "But I do have a box for you if you don't mind waiting a moment." She rose from her seat

119

and maneuvered her way past the velvet rope to meet Bess in the foyer.

"Now wait a minute. Stop. I want to know why you didn't tell me you were Tam Gillis's aunt."

"When would I have told you that, dear? The boy wasn't arrested until after I saw you last."

Bess started to speak but stopped herself. The old woman was right. "But you knew I was looking into the murders. You should have come to me. You had no way of knowing I'd speak with Tam." The words sounded hollow in her ears. She hadn't really admitted to herself that she was looking into the murders, but what else could she really call it at this point? She was here, wasn't she?

"I'm under very strict orders from the fine officers of Antioch to keep my mouth shut about these murders. I know things that they don't want the general public knowing. Officer Howland told me he'd arrest me for obstruction." Winnie's smile was gone. Her eyes were stern now, afraid.

"You don't think he'd really do that, though, do you?" Bess tried to imagine Winnie Tate locked up and the absurdity of it nearly made her laugh. "The press would eat them alive."

"I don't take chances like that. What you wish to do is your business. But I certainly did try to let you know certain things."

"You mean about the dragon?"

"No, I mean about Tam." She leaned in and muttered under her breath, "Where did you think those notes were coming from?"

Bess felt numb. Her mind whirled, thinking back to all the strange occurrences she'd experienced over the last few days.

ANTIOCH

"I told you, I'm not supposed to be talking about any of this," Winnie said.

"Did you call my house?"

Winnie blinked, the anger in Bess's voice seemed to physically wound her. "I . . . did, yes."

"And what about the bathroom at my work yesterday?"

"I don't know what you're talking about."

"Oh, the fuck you don't." Bess felt a twinge of guilt for cussing. "I'm sorry. But I'm going around feeling like a mad woman, thinking I'm losing my mind, and the only thing I'm being haunted by is an old lady."

"If you'd please take the box I have for you." Winnie walked away, heading to retrieve the box of Tam's notes.

"No way. I'm done with this. I don't care anymore. Do you hear me? I don't care."

"But you have to help us," Winnie said.

"But I don't," Bess shot back. "I wish I'd never come here. You've been using me ever since you met me. Manipulating me. I'm done. Find someone else to haunt."

Bess turned her back on Winnie Tate and felt her old eyes burning into her, but she didn't care. Disappointing a woman she barely knew shouldn't even register on her scale of moral wrongdoings. And if Tam truly was innocent, then it was for the cops to find out, or the judge, or the jury. Anyone but her. Scott Howland had been telling her from the first day they met that she should stop interfering in his investigation and she was finally ready to listen.

ON THE WAY home Bess stopped by The Hole to talk with Carol. The shop was pretty busy. All of the barstools were full and Bess noticed four or five customers browsing among the books and gifts. Saturdays were good for business. The fluorescent lighting made a pleasant hum overhead and the place smelled of beer and books. There was nothing quite like evenings at the bookstore.

"The boss is behind the bar, if you're looking," Lucy said from over near the cash register.

"Thanks, I was. Although it looks like she's got a crowd." Bess smiled at Lucy, making an effort to not hate her.

"The woman is magic. Every time she bartends the place fills up like a landfill."

"That's some pleasant imagery." Bess rolled her eyes.

"Some days it feels more fitting than others. Some of these people are total garbage." Lucy shrugged.

"Well, maybe don't call them garbage to their faces."

"Hey, no problem, boss."

Lucy saluted her before walking away, ending Bess's obligation to make polite conversation. Bess resisted the instinct to ask a customer if they needed any help. She wasn't on the clock and, despite the devotion she felt to this place, it wasn't her business, which meant giving away her time for free was a fool's game. Instead, she walked over to the bar and stood at the corner. The hectic atmosphere suited Carol. She seemed younger when she was busy. A loose tendril of curly auburn hair hung in her eyes and she absently swiped at it with the back of her hand as she made drinks and conversation at a rapid pace. She was smiling freely, something Bess rarely saw Carol do, and the effect was charming. In moments like this it was obvious why Carol opened a bookstore. She loved the work, she loved the people.

When she finally spotted Bess she gave a quick little wave and motioned for her to come behind the bar.

"What are you doing here?"

"I was out and thought I'd drop in, see how you were."

"I'm great. Business is fantastic tonight. I think it's the weather."

Bess glanced outside and tried to imagine what Carol meant about the weather. It'd been hot and rainy, but she wasn't positive how that translated into sales. "Do you need any help?"

"Hell no, you enjoy your night off. I've got this covered. Oh but, I did mean to tell you," she said, swatting at the stray curl again. "A cop came in a little bit ago, he said he knew you. Something Holland?"

"Howland?"

"Yes, that's it. He had a drink and said you recommended the place. Is he the guy you were out with the other night?"

"No, that was someone else. Detective Howland is just . . . someone I know."

"He's nice looking. You should get to know him better." Carol dropped a very un-Carol-like wink and Bess laughed.

"I don't know how I feel about him. He's attractive, but he's also . . . "

"A cop?"

"Yeah, that sums it up."

"He seemed nice," Carol said, but her attention was already somewhere else.

"Look, I'm going to get out of here. I felt like seeing you," Bess said.

Carol stopped what she was doing and studied her friend's face. "You sure? Why don't you stay for a drink? Hell, I'll even drive you home if you want. This rush is going to end any minute and I'll be sitting here twiddling my thumbs wishing I had my Bess around."

"You've always got your Lucy," Bess laughed.

"I mean it, sit down. We don't get to talk enough anymore."

Bess rolled her eyes and pretended to be put out. There was something beautiful about someone asking you to stay with them. About the offer without prompt. And even when there was a prompt, or clues to a prompt, at least they loved you enough to notice and care. Because caring was no longer a given in the world. Despite the great universal interconnection of all things, people had still, by and large, chosen not to care. Even if it meant—and oh god, it very likely did—their destruction.

Why did people believe Amelia Earhart was a spy? Was it because the evidence was there? Or because they wanted to give her a greater purpose? To imagine her out there, the great female aviator, done in and lost to history by a stupid navigational error, it almost hurt too much to breathe. But lost on a secret spy mission from FDR—the possibilities were vast and majestic and worth dying for. Die a hero, Amelia, not a failure. Die a hero or a bank teller or a fairy tale in a young girl's notebook. Or all these things and more.

Carol eased up to the curb in front of Bess's house and shut off the engine. They'd agreed that Carol would pick her up for work in the morning and she could retrieve her car then. No problem. The store didn't open until noon on Sundays, plenty of time to sleep off a few drinks and be fresh for work. Bess peered up the walkway at her darkened house and exhaled slowly, like she wanted to get every bit of oxygen out of her body.

"Doesn't look very inviting, does it?"

"Are your windows muddy?" Carol asked.

"It's a long story. I'm being stalked by a little old lady."

"Yeah, that does sound like a long story. Hey, when was the last time we had a sleepover?"

Bess rolled her head over to look at her boss and friend. "We have literally never done that."

"All the more reason we should. We can say it's a team building exercise. Oh hell, if we order a pizza I can write it off on my taxes."

"Are you being serious?"

"Yeah. I mean, I don't have to sleep on your couch if you're not into it, but it could be fun to come in and talk some more. Unless I'm not welcome." Carol exaggerated the last sentence, making it over the top so she could play it all off as a joke if Bess said no. She could leave without any exposed feelings.

"Carol, you're always welcome," Bess said.

Bess exited the car and pulled her keys from her pocket. She shook them in her hand until the door key dislodged itself from the pack. She briefly wondered if there was anything inside the house she needed to clean up before Carol got in there. Not dirty dishes or clothes, Carol wouldn't judge her housekeeping. But maybe notes on saints or Amelia Earhart or a bunch of murdered women.

She flicked on the light as soon as she entered and scanned the top of her desk for anything too weird for company. But most of her notes were out in the garage and that seemed like a safe enough place for them to stay.

"Welcome to my humble abode," she said, gesturing for Carol to enter with a grand flail of her arm. "Can I get you a drink? I only have Fat Tire and orange juice. And I guess tap water."

"I'll take a beer if you don't mind," Carol replied, taking a seat on the couch. "So, what's up with this old lady stalker that smears mud on your walls?"

ANTIOCH

"Nope," Bess said, retrieving two beers and plopping down next to Carol. "You already think I'm a nutbag."

"I in no way think of you as a scrotum, dear. I'm worried that the homeowner's association is going to start sending you nasty letters."

"The neighbors are already complaining." Bess nodded solemnly.

"Is there something I should worry about? Is the little old lady going to break in?"

"I'd like to tell you it wasn't possible, but I honestly can't." Bess giggled as she opened her beer. Why shouldn't she tell Carol everything? She already thought Bess was slipping. Was letting her know about Amy Eckhardt really going to change much?

Her phone rang and she pulled it out of her pocket. The caller ID showed *Anonymous*.

"Hello?" she said, rolling her eyes and mouthing *telemarketer* at Carol.

"Have you been talking to the cops about me?" Not a telemarketer.

"Greg? Is that you?"

"Of course it's me. I heard you were down at the police station. That you're getting cozy with that fuckwad detective."

"Well, first off, hey, nice to hear from you. I'm flattered that you called," Bess said, affecting a Southern accent she didn't normally have.

"You listen to me, you little bitch." There was venom in his voice. "I've got enough problems without you going around town telling everyone I killed my girlfriend."

"I don't know what you're talking about." Bess hung up before he could say anything else.

127

"What was that about?" Carol asked. "I didn't even hear it ring."

"Yeah, I keep the volume down," Bess said.

"Was the telemarketer named Greg?"

Bess sighed. "It wasn't a telemarketer. Greg is the guy I had a date with. He's been, well, he's been sort of a handful."

Bess told Carol the story of her date with Greg and the SOS message she received from Amelia Earhart—*Amy Eckhardt*. She tried to swerve away from anything too unexplainable. Anything that seemed even remotely supernatural. Not only because she wanted Carol to believe her, but because she feared that if she said those things out loud, really thought about them, she might truly go as insane as she probably already seemed.

"And turns out this weird old lady has been trying to low-key manipulate me into becoming Matlock," she finished.

Carol was silent. She'd finished her beer and helped herself to another one while Bess spoke. Bess didn't blame her. The story basically required alcohol.

"And Lucy is convinced the guy is innocent?" Carol finally asked.

"Yeah. That was truly the strangest part for me, too."

"Lucy's a good judge of character. That's all."

"Sis real woke. I know."

Carol stayed silent and Bess started peeling the label off her bottle, slowly at first, until she had it cleanly removed.

"What I don't understand is how this person could be sending these messages through your radio," Carol said.

ANTIOCH

"You and me both. For all I know it's some elaborate scheme to drive me crazy. But honestly, I don't know why anyone would care enough about me to want to drive me crazy."

"You make it seem really pathetic."

"It is."

"Bess, I don't mean to go where I'm not wanted, but how did your life get like this? All this loner stuff. You're too young to be so isolated."

"Shit, I don't know. After high school most of my friends went away to college and never came back. That's small-town life. I worked and attended community college and minded my own business." Bess felt satisfied with this answer, but Carol was eyeing her suspiciously.

"That's not all of it though."

"Then you tell me."

"I mean, you were engaged a couple years ago. And then it all just . . . I don't know what. It all disappeared."

A sudden flush of shame and anger swelled inside Bess. This whole having-people-over-to-her-house thing was turning out to be a pain in the ass. "That didn't work out," Bess said quietly.

"That much is obvious," Carol said. "But what no one knows is, why? One day you're getting married and the next POOF! Brandon's gone. And not just gone from the house—gone from Antioch."

"We wanted different things," Bess said.

"We'd all heard the rumors, Bess. That he was screwing around. Did he leave with one of them?"

"That's enough. We aren't doing this."

129

Carol held up her hands in surrender. "Okay, okay. I was only saying. You weren't always a loner."

"Great, cool. Can you mind your fucking business now?"

"Wow, just because your ex was screwing half a dozen other women, there's no need to snap at me."

The two glared at each other in silence, neither ready to admit they'd been too harsh. A knock on the door made them both jump. Carol even let out a high yelp that would have been funny any other time. Bess glanced down at her phone, waiting for it to ring like it had before, waiting for the demon voices to start pouring in. It remained dark and unassuming.

"Do you think it's that Greg guy?" Carol asked.

"I have no idea," Bess replied heading for the door. The porch was dark and she didn't bother with the light. In one fast motion she pulled open the door and scanned the yard slamming it shut again.

"Did you see anything?" Carol asked.

"Not a thing. Which isn't unusual."

Bess opened the door again, slower this time, and scanned the yard. She stepped out and swore as she banged her bare toes into something on the stoop. There was a large cardboard box nestled against the doorstep. Taped to the top was a piece of stationary that proudly proclaimed its origin as the Antioch Historical Society. Bess picked it up and read it out loud to Carol.

"'Bess—I deeply regret causing you stress. It was never my intention. Please take these notebooks. You're the only person who can help Tam. Sincerely, Winnie Tate.'"

"You've got to be kidding," Carol said.

ANTIOCH

Bess hefted the box into the entryway and closed the door behind her. The flaps were not folded down, so she could already see the papers and notebooks neatly arranged inside.

"How did that old lady even carry that up here?" Carol asked.

"Least of my worries," Bess responded, pulling out the first book. It was a thick, 5-subject spiral bound with a plain black paper cover that was pulling away from the spirals. On the inside of the cover someone, presumably Tam Gillis, has written the name Ashley Bunkirk.

The first pages were filled with a detailed biography of the dead girl. There were notes on how she looked, where she ate, where she lived. He even had information on her parents and close friends.

"This looks more like evidence that he definitely, for sure killed her," Carol said, peering over Bess's shoulder. "The little freak was a stalker."

Some of the phrases were highlighted. Things like "ate at Morning Glory Café" and "used to work at movie theater." Bess flipped to the second section of the notebook and read the heading: "'Brandy Leroy.'"

"She was the third victim," Carol said.

This section was much like the first, Brandy's life story, in as much mundane detail as possible. Brandy also ate at the café, but as far as Bess could tell, she'd never worked at a movie theater. Brandy had been a nail technician. She lived alone. Her parents were both dead—victims of a freak car accident when Brandy was twenty.

The other sections of the book outlined the lives of the other women claimed by the Impaler. The more

Bess read, the more uneasy she felt. It was like reading someone else's diary. And none of it exactly spelled Tam's innocence. Carol was right, it made him look guilty.

"Where's the first one?" Bess wondered aloud. "This notebook starts with Ashley, she was the second victim. So if he's the killer, or just an avid biographer, where's number one?"

"I can't even remember her name," Carol said.

Bess knelt next to the box and started pulling out the contents—loose papers, notebooks, photographs, even maps. There was an orange notebook about halfway down. On the cover he'd used an eraser to etch a ghostly white number one. The name Margot Cooper was printed neatly on the first page.

"That was it," Carol said. "Margot."

"Sounds a lot like Margaret," Bess said.

"Not exactly."

"But real close."

Margot had been twenty-three years old when she died. She was a self-taught culinary whiz and worked as a chef at a local steak house called Farber's. She was single, but often went out with her co-workers at the end of the night to close down bars and dance. Margot's parents were devout Baptists and Margot attended regular services as well as Bible study twice a week. On her days off, Margot would head out early for breakfast at the Morning Glory Café, in the afternoon she would watch a movie, whatever the cheap matinee happened to be, or window shop. She had a gym membership, but rarely used it. She almost never ate at home, preferring instead to have her meals out in public—often alone—where she would usually receive free food from her culinary friends. She had thick blonde hair, generally pulled back into a ponytail, and light brown eyes.

"She sounds nice," Bess said.

"Isn't that the same church Wayne goes to?"

"I think so, yeah."

"This feels so ugly."

Bess nodded.

"You should call the cops."

"I'm not going to do that."

"This is clearly evidence. The guy was stalking every single one of these women. With these notebooks they could throw out that hokey confession all together. No jury on the planet would say he was innocent."

"Is that what we want?" Bess asked. "I don't know that he's guilty. But I know the cops sure want him to be. I give them this and the case is shut for good and we never find Amy."

"Do you really think you can find her?" Carol asked.

"I really don't know."

Bess pulled another spiral notebook from the pile and opened it to another profile: Daniel Mills.

She skimmed the small neat print for the highlighted passages. This time, each highlight corresponded with something she'd seen in the profiles of the victims.

"Do you think this could be a suspect?' Bess asked.

Carol raised an eyebrow. "You know exactly what I think. This is police work—not the job of a bookseller."

Bess frowned and kept reading. There were

snapshots stuck in with some of the passages, what appeared to be surveillance photos—taken from around corners and over the tops of tables. Covert.

"Tam was following this guy," Bess said.

"The same way he was following all the victims."

"But he didn't have photos of any of them. Nothing like this. He's got dates and times. He was definitely tailing him for some reason."

"You know what? I think I'm tired. I'm going to head home."

"What? Are you serious?" Bess couldn't believe what she was hearing. They'd been delivered the most exciting package possible, and Carol wanted to leave.

Carol's eyes were steady and dry. "I've had enough of this. I don't want it."

"I'm sorry," Bess said, although she didn't know what she was apologizing for. For telling Carol all her secrets, for involving her in this. "But you can't tell the police. I'll tell them myself if I feel like I should. But not yet. Let me do it my way."

"What happens when your way gets you killed?" Carol asked.

"It won't happen."

Carol left a short time later, promising to return the next morning as planned. Bess lay down across her couch and pulled a blanket up around her face. She'd never felt so incredibly alone. She'd had a partner for an entire hour. Someone in this mess with her instead of the sea of people against her. She hadn't realized how good it would feel to share everything. How much she needed to unload.

Carol was her boss first. And maybe Bess had blurred that line a little too much today; blurred it past Carol's comfort zone, certainly. Bess swallowed hard and told herself she wasn't going to cry. She hadn't lost anything today.

In fact, she'd gained something. Now she had the box of notes, and as angry as she was with Winnie, she couldn't help but feel compelled by it. The profiles of the victims were damning, but Bess didn't believe they were the notes of a stalker any more than her notes out in the garage were the ravings of a mad woman. If she believed she wasn't crazy, and for whatever reason she still did, then she was willing to extend that same leniency to Tam Gillis and Winnie Tate.

The maps inside the box were mainly road maps of Antioch he'd printed off from Google or Yahoo. They contained little red ink symbols with a key beneath to tell you what each represented. Margot Cooper found. Ashley Bunkirk found. Brandy Leroy found. Emily Baker found. Olivia Terry found. Bethany Ladd found. Bess could see no correlations connecting the dots.

On a separate map he'd plotted out key points for Daniel Mills. Where he lived and banked and ate and worked. Bess glanced back and forth between the "found" map and the Daniel Mills map, but again saw no patterns. She wondered if Tam saw something she didn't, or if he'd also been disappointed.

Bess spent the night on her couch reading over the lives of the six victims. But mostly she read about Daniel Mills. Daniel was the leader of the young adult's ministry at First Baptist of Antioch—the same church Margot Cooper and her family attended. The same Bible study Wayne kept inviting her to. During the week he worked in the lawn and garden section of Lowe's. And if he used his employee discount to buy PVC pipes, well, the bio Bess had in front of her didn't mention it. He lived alone and didn't have any relatives in Antioch. He'd moved here nine years ago, when he was thirty-four, and immediately joined the church. This appeared to be his only true social circle.

Bess had been careful to set plenty of alarms for herself in case she fell asleep so Carol wouldn't catch her off guard in the morning. She was dressed and guzzling coffee when a car pulled up in front of her home. But it wasn't Carol's dark blue compact. Instead it was a bright green hybrid that Bess wished she didn't recognize.

Lucy was out of the car and up the drive before Bess had a chance to rinse her coffee cup in the sink and grab her purse. She lightly tapped and called, "Knock knock," rising up on her tippy toes to look through the glass at the top of the door. Bess yanked it open, purposely hoping to knock Lucy over. Not hurt her. No, nothing too serious.

"Yikes," Lucy exclaimed, stumbling back a couple steps. "Sorry, Carol asked me if I could get you. She's not feeling good I guess—blah blah. Here I am!"

"Here you are," Bess said, smiling. Carol had clearly felt too uncomfortable after last night to come back to Bess's house. Bess set her jaw in stony defiance against the feelings that tried to well up inside her.

ANTIOCH

Once they were in the car, Bess closed her eyes and said a silent prayer to Saint Margaret that they could pass the time in silence.

"Wayne told me you were going to talk to Tam Gillis."

Fucking good for nothing saints. "Did he?"

"He sure did. Now tell me everything. Do you think he's innocent? Because you know I do." Lucy was a morning person like no other.

"I really don't know what I think. I needed to see for myself, you know?"

"Absolutely. I totally get it. Do you have any theories? You know, about who really did it?"

"Why? Do you have theories?"

"I have more theories than I can count at this point. I was talking to Carol about it this morning."

"Before or after she asked you to pick me up?"

"Uh, it was before, I think. No, I'm sure. Before," Lucy answered.

Bess smiled. Carol wasn't avoiding her, she was trying to set her up with someone more her type. "What's your best theory?" she asked.

"My suspect number one is Hector Bowman," Lucy said proudly.

"Hector, as in our UPS driver?" Bess asked.

"Absolutely, he's creepy. He's got that big truck; he could be hiding anything in there."

"UPS isn't exactly a small business; other people load his truck. And he has to stick to a tight schedule. Pretty sure he doesn't get to drive the truck in his down time either."

It was taking longer than usual to get to the bookstore. Traffic in Antioch had changed from nonexistent to a nuisance. Not only had the media rolled in, but the news had brought with it a strange sort of tourist. Serial killer enthusiasts were having unofficial walking tours through downtown. Bess wondered if Winnie was seeing an uptick in visitors at the historical society. It seemed murder was good for the economy.

"You have to admit he's a creep."

"He's a pervert," Bess said. "I can't deny that. But I'm not positive that makes him a murderer. Who else do you have in mind?"

"Well, I'm not sure." Lucy was sulking. "I'd really been thinking it was Hector." Lucy was quiet for a minute before she continued. "Really anyone with a truck could do it. I mean, local plumbers—they'd have access to lots of PVC pipe, right? Is that what PVC pipe is for? Plumbing?"

Bess didn't respond. Lucy didn't have any real theories, she was grasping at straws.

Bess headed for Carol's office as soon as she arrived, but Carol was nowhere in sight. She called her cell phone, but only got her voicemail. She was being ignored after all, but it was less likely because of the events of the night before, and more because she didn't want to hear Bess complain about being picked up by Lucy.

"I have to go out for a little bit," Bess told Lucy. "Errands. Will you be okay on your own? I can call Wayne in if you want."

"No way, Wayne doesn't work Sundays, you know that. It's his family day."

"Right. I forgot. But you're cool, right?"

Lucy rolled her eyes. "Sure, Bess, why not."

"Don't be that way, you know I'd let you go if you needed to."

Lucy didn't say anything for a few long seconds. Finally she shook her head and stalked away.

"God damn attitude," Bess muttered as she headed out the door.

She walked all the way to the jail and arrived out of breath. There were more reporters on the sidewalk this time and Bess did her best not to make eye contact with anyone as she slunk inside.

This time the cops were a little more prepared for a visitor, although they still eyed her with some fascination.

"Two visits in a week? You got a thing for inmates?" the guard asked her.

"Fuck off," Bess replied.

"Nah, I've heard about that, ladies who get off on psycho killers. It's a disease." He opened the door to the same room she'd been in before. This time Tam was already inside. "This is not a conjugal visit, lovebirds. Keep it PG in here."

"Did you get the notes?" Tam asked as soon as the door was closed.

"Did it ever occur to you that those notes make you seem incredibly guilty?"

"Of course, that's why I gave them to you and not the police."

"Let's skip the part where I ask you a million questions to prove you're not actually a stalker asshole and assume I believe you, or at the very least feel okay believing you because you're locked up in here."

"Sounds good to me, I guess," Tam said. "So, what do we do now?"

"Why Daniel Mills? What brought you to him?" Bess asked.

"Wow, okay. Yeah, he's my favorite in all this. There were a couple other suspects early on, but Daniel, Daniel's the one I like for it."

"Brilliant. But I need to know why."

"It's the church. See, I read this thing that with serial killers like this, they usually start with someone they know. They know the first victim and they like it or they don't get what they need from it and they go from there."

"Where did you read this?"

"I guess I saw it, really. Um, that movie *Zodiac*? With Jake Gyllenhaal?"

"Never mind. Forget I asked. Just . . . just tell me why it's Mills." Bess reminded herself that Tam was basically a child playing detective the only way he knew how—by watching murder movies on basic cable. And who was she to judge? She was playing detective by listening to a kid who got his ideas from David Fincher movies.

"Okay, so Mills attended the same church as Margot Cooper. Her parents still go there, but Margot actually stopped about a month before she disappeared. Margot was in Mills's young adult study group on Monday and Wednesday nights. And by all accounts, he was pretty in love with her."

"What accounts?" Bess asked, praying he would not bring up Jake Gyllenhaal.

"Her friends, her parents."

"You talked to her parents?"

"Oh yeah, they were happy to talk to me, thrilled actually. I mean, I guess they're less thrilled now. In fact, talking to them probably doesn't look so good for me now . . . looking back . . . ."

"Focus. I don't have all day for this. If he had a thing for her, why didn't the police check him out?"

"They did for a second. I mean, they basically checked out the whole town right at first. Cast a big net, you know? But they ruled him out because he was supposedly at work when she was kidnapped."

"So then how'd he do it? Was Jesus his copilot?"

"That's funny. I like that. But no, no. The cops have the timeline wrong. They don't really know *when* she was kidnapped. All they have is an approximate time of when she was last seen and when her parents reported her missing. They've got no way to know when she was abducted. And the time of death is even worse. That head was pretty decayed, and of course she was killed somewhere else, no clue where, so they don't know if there were accelerants for the decay. So the real timeline is more like a twenty-four-hour window of abduction, time of death—fucking forget it—it's like a possible month long window. The smallest window is the placement of the head in that lot. Had to have been between two a.m. and five a.m. And nobody—I mean *nobody*—has an alibi for *that* timeframe."

"Stop. This doesn't make logical sense. Why would the cops discount someone as having an alibi if they don't really know when she was abducted?"

"Because they're cops, Bess. They're fucking useless. But also because someone said they saw a woman who matches her description getting into a vehicle at seven p.m. the day she went missing."

"And you don't think that was her?"

"I mean, it coulda been. But I don't think that's who kidnapped her. Margot was popular enough. Margot had friends. She could have been with anyone at 7 p.m. on a Friday. That's no big deal."

"I see your point," Bess said.

"Glad someone does." Tam smiled at her and Bess was struck again by how truly young he looked. "Okay, here's what you need to know—Mills matches up with every single woman. I swear. But he actually knew Margot. The best contact I had was Margot's best friend, Cherish McKenzie. She'll talk to you. I'm sure of it. She was scared of Daniel Mills."

"Will she talk to the cops?"

Tam considered. "Probably not. She doesn't trust that detective."

"Howland."

"Yep, she said she knew him."

"Okay, I'll talk to Cherish McKenzie and find out what I can about Mills. Do you know her number?"

"Of course. But be careful. Daniel knew I was following him."

CHERISH HAD SOUNDED eager to talk when Bess called her. It felt too easy, but Bess was grateful for something easy. They were meeting at the Morning Glory Café where Tam had worked before his arrest. Cherish said she and Tam had always gone there in the past and she felt comfortable with the location.

The café closed early on Sundays, so Bess called Lucy and asked her to close up for her. Lucy had whined a little, but eventually relented. What else could she do? Bess didn't like leaving her alone all day, but they'd be dead most of the time, anyway. Wayne wasn't the only person in Antioch who considered Sunday to be a family day.

When Bess entered the café there were no other patrons. She strolled to the counter and ordered a large black coffee and added her own cream and sugar at a small station set up to the right of the cash register. Bess carried her coffee over to a small table in the corner where she felt like they would have some privacy. She obsessively checked her phone for messages or calls until a petite young woman came through the doors and smiled at her.

"Are you Bess?"

"I am." She stood to meet her. "Cherish?"

"That's me, yeah." Cherish awkwardly reached to shake Bess's hand. She couldn't have been taller than five feet and Bess had the absurd impulse to squat slightly. Instead she sat back down. "Sorry about making you come out here, but I can't be too careful."

"I completely understand. I don't know you either." Bess smiled in a way she hoped was reassuring, but was probably a little manic. "Do you want to get something?" She motioned toward the counter.

"Nah, I'm good. I can't stay too long."

"Oh sure." Bess took a deep breath and plunged straight in. "Well, I guess I'm looking for how Daniel Mills knew your friend. How he knew Margot."

"Tam probably told you they met through church. And that's true. But Margot told me he used to come by her house a lot too. He asked her out, which was sort of . . . well, he was older. And he looks normal enough, but the dude's a little backward, you know?" Cherish's dark brown eyes kept cutting from side to side. "So Margot tells him she isn't interested in anything like that. Well, then he shows up at her front door with flowers telling her momma that they got a date that night. Margot 'bout died. She tells him to leave, but he won't. Her daddy finally had to ask him to leave. He walks him out and everything."

"You're kidding? Is that when she stopped going to church?"

"No, she was still going. But he kept pulling her aside and asking her why she wouldn't date him. And . . . Margot said he got a little out of hand. Like eventually he stops asking her out and starts asking her to touch him, you know?"

"I do, yeah." Bess felt sick inside. Act One. Margot of Antioch spurns the advances of Daniel.

"Eventually she left the church. She couldn't keep being there with him. And then, well, you know the rest." Cherish looked over her shoulder at the large windows and surveyed the people passing by outside.

"I can't believe the police didn't follow up on this guy. He seems like an obvious suspect."

"I don't trust those cops, anyway," Cherish mumbled, glancing back at the door.

"Oh yeah, Tam told me you knew Detective Howland. That you didn't trust him."

"Yeah. You could say I know him. We dated for about two years." Cherish laughed.

Bess was shocked. She wasn't prepared for the twinge of jealousy that slithered down into her belly. "I had no idea."

"Well, I'm not exactly bragging. That man wouldn't listen to me even if the department *wasn't* crooked."

"What do you mean by 'crooked'?"

Cherish laughed. "Don't tell me you think little ole Antioch is some kinda Mayberry. Because, sister, it's not so. Think about it, outside of this serial killer shit, do you ever hear about any real crime in this town? Ya don't. And I'm here to tell you it ain't because it don't happen. It's because they make it go away."

"How's that? How can they *make* crime go away?"

Bess fully regretted talking to Cherish at this point. The last thing she needed was more wacko conspiracy theories when she already had a whole box full waiting for her at home.

"There's lots of ways. There's what they're doing to Tam, framing an innocent kid. And if a cop commits a crime, well, it really isn't a crime."

"Yes, it is," Bess said.

"Don't tell *me!* Tell *them.* Or really don't, because you seem sweet and I don't want you disappearing," Cherish said.

Bess nodded. She felt numb and naïve and ridiculous. How was she supposed to be catching a god damned serial killer when the idea of crooked cops left her speechless?

"Do you have any proof? Or am I just supposed to believe you?" Bess asked.

"What kind of proof would make you feel better? You think if I had solid proof, I'd be meeting you and not those reporters out there?"

"Maybe talking to a reporter is exactly what we should be doing."

Cherish laughed. "I'm not trying to bring trouble down like that. The cops like having a nice low-crime city. It makes them look good, it keeps people complacent. No one asks questions when they think things are fine. And all this goes back to why Tam is going to be locked up forever and Daniel Mills is going to keep killing people. Tam asked too many questions."

"But when the killings continue, the public will know they have the wrong man," Bess said.

"Maybe. Maybe not. Maybe then it's a copycat.

Shit, I don't know. It's not my job to think like they do. But what I know for sure is that the only way to get the cops to say they have the wrong man is to give them hard evidence they can't ignore. Show them something they can't possibly brush off. They'll call you crazy if you let them. Don't let them."

"Do you have any ideas how I do that without also getting myself killed?" Bess asked.

"I absolutely don't. Which is why I'm not doing it."

"I know Tam was following Mills. But he obviously couldn't find anything. I don't know what more I can do."

"Then my advice is to leave it alone. Take care of yourself." Cherish shrugged. "I like Tam, he's a little sweetie. But I'm not going to prison in his place."

"I can't ignore it. This isn't only about Tam, someone's got Amy Eckhardt. She could still be alive. If there's even a chance, I need to try."

"Amy, yeah. Tam thought maybe Vlad had her. I don't know, she could be a runaway. It happens."

"Amy didn't run away," Bess said.

Bess finished her coffee and said goodbye to Cherish. Talking to her had left Bess even more confused. She hadn't necessarily trusted Howland before, but she hadn't suspected the whole department was involved in a cover up. And she didn't like how much the thought of him with Cherish hurt her feelings.

Bess drove home in silence. She kept imagining Amelia Earhart. Not crashed on the shores of some deserted island, but still in the air, circling. She imagined the fear rising slowly inside her as her fuel levels got lower and lower. Radioing for help, miserably off course, lost and uncertain. Did Fred know how scared she was? Or was it he who panicked first? Bess imagined she kept herself together in the air—she felt safer there, more at ease, more capable of survival. That it wasn't until she was trapped on land that her fear overtook her. Bess didn't know where her safe spaces were anymore.

The house was lit up when she arrived and she couldn't remember if she'd left the lights on or if she should be concerned, and honestly, she no longer cared. Too much had happened for a few lights to worry her much. Nothing in the house seemed out of order.

Bess considered what Cherish had told her. For the police to help, she had to bring them undeniable proof. She had to bring them something tangible they couldn't turn a blind eye to. She would need to catch him in the act. Or find Amy alive. Both options seemed terrifying.

According to Tam's notes, Daniel's young adult classes met on Mondays and Wednesdays at 6 p.m. She could attend tomorrow and see him firsthand. Before she started outright stalking, she thought it might be a good idea to know the man, see if she even thought he was capable of being a killer. She wasn't willing to discount her own intuition simply because she might be losing her mind.

There were still a few of Tam's notebooks left in the box and Bess pulled them out and made neat stacks on the carpet. Then one in particular caught her eye. The name on the front read "Greg Leeds."

"What's this bullshit?"

The notebook was different from the others.

ANTIOCH

Where they had been basic spiral bound with paper covers, this was a fully bound hardcover journal with a deep blue cover and metallic gold roses growing up the sides. She saw the name "Greg Leeds" written on the side in some sort of white ink. The inside was full of soft cream-colored pages.

Bess opened the book expecting to see the same style of profile as all the other books. She wasn't far off. It included where he lived and worked, his routines. There was a physical description of him as well as a crude drawing of his face. It even had her date with him noted, a fact that made her skin crawl. Amy wasn't mentioned until close to the end.

Tam must have thought Greg was a possible suspect in the disappearance of Amy, if not all the murders. She thought back to the phone call she received the night before. Greg definitely had anger issues. But anger didn't make him a murderer. Of course, neither did hitting on a young woman at your church.

She was spinning in circles. Running on empty. She knew the crash was imminent. Bess trudged into her bedroom, kicked her clothes off into the corner, and slid under the covers naked; she didn't have the energy for pajamas. Within minutes she'd fallen down into a deep and dreamless sleep.

11

THE KNOCKING ON the door wasn't like in her dreams. It was insistent. It was a banging. It was painful. Bess sat up in bed and scooped the blankets up around her, trying to bring the world into focus. Slowly, without any urgency, she rose from bed and dug a pair of jeans and a tee shirt out of her closet.

By the time she reached the door the knocking was a constant ramming of fist against wood. She opened it without any hesitation. Greg Leeds stood on her front stoop. His blond hair was falling into his face and there was sweat on his brow.

"Can I help you?" she asked him.

"Why won't you answer the phone?" His voice was a degree below hysteria.

"Pretty sure I blocked your number. Was there something you needed?"

He started to walk into the house and Bess came alive for a moment, her arm shooting out to block his path. Greg glared down at her and fear began to stir low in her gut and for a moment she was glad for it. She was thankful for emotion the way you were glad when the pins and needles started up in your arm after sleeping on it all night, because it hurt, but it wasn't dead. The pain meant you were still alive.

"I need to come in." He took another step forward, his body now against hers, and Bess realized they were not truly alone. It was him and her and a gun in between them. She stared down at it, stunned by how small it seemed, how foreign. "I need to come in," he repeated.

Bess stood aside and let him push his way into her home. She didn't want him there, but it wasn't worth dying over. "What do you want?"

"You said you could hear Amy. You told me she was talking to you through the radio."

Bess nodded. Her mouth was so dry. She thought about getting a glass of water, but she wasn't sure if that was allowed. She didn't know the rules of being a hostage. She assumed sudden movements were out of the question. The thought caught her off guard. Was that what she was? A *hostage?*

"I want to hear. I want to know what she's saying."

"It doesn't work like that, Greg. I can't just . . . she's not broadcasting at a regular time. I can't tune into NPR at ten and six and catch her latest show."

"Try. That's all. Please." Something in Greg's face changed. A new emotion twisted his features and made him seem pitiable instead of someone she should fear. Grief infected him and made him weak. "I need to hear her again."

"Will you put the gun down?"

"No," he whispered.

"Okay," Bess said. "I'll try." She walked to the garage door, forcing her back to stay straight and her steps to be even. No sudden movements. No weakness.

She turned to her radio, flicked it on, rolled the dial to static and stepped back. "This is where she usually finds me. In the static."

Greg looked at her like he was trying to decide if she was lying or teasing him. Finally, he must have decided she wasn't or that it didn't matter. He turned his attention to the radio and waited.

"I don't know that she's going to talk. She doesn't always. I don't make this happen."

"Just shut up," he yelled at her. His voice cracked with emotion, but Bess didn't know if it was grief or lunacy. She stood in silence and watched Greg pace the concrete floor, his eyes trained on the radio. She thought she might be able to catch him off guard, tackle him and get the gun. But he was so tightly wound, his nerves on such high alert, that she feared she might get shot in the face if she moved too quickly. She stayed still and waited.

The transmission came through as a whisper at first, slowly building in intensity.

Act One. Margaret of Antioch spurns the advances of Olybrius.

Act Two. Margaret of Antioch is tortured.

Act Three. Margaret of Antioch is swallowed by a dragon.

Act Four. Saint Margaret of Antioch is

disgorged by the dragon.

Act Five. Saint Margaret of Antioch is beheaded.

"What the fuck is this?" he asked Bess.

"I don't know. I've heard it before. It's a recording or something. It just repeats."

"That's not Amy."

"No, but I think it's connected. Let it go for a few minutes."

He frowned at Bess but didn't challenge her.

After five verses of the Ballad of Saint Margaret the recording began to break up and fade out. Static rose again.

"I need you to know, I didn't do this," Greg said.

"Do what?"

"Kidnap Amy! I'm not a killer, Bess. I don't know what she's been saying about me, but I swear I'm not a killer."

"What who's been saying about you?"

"*Amy.* She's always looking at things the wrong way. God damn Amy. She's the type who would see someone killed in self-defense and call it murder."

"What was self-defense? What happened to Amy?"

"What? No, don't twist my words. Don't you dare. This isn't about me. I didn't do anything." He was pacing again, his eyes going back and forth between Bess and the radio, the radio and Bess.

"It's about Vlad the Impaler, right?" Bess asked.

"Sure it is. You know, I wonder what he calls himself. Don't serial killers always want to name themselves?

153

Zodiac. BTK. This guy never named himself." She liked it better when he was talking.

"You're a lousy detective, Bess. I mean it. You're absolutely terrible at this." Greg rubbed his free hand across his mouth, pinching his bottom lip, stretching it out like a fish. "You were in the historical society with that old woman the same as I was. You heard her say what was on the wall. The Dragon. He's the Dragon, come back to take his revenge on Margaret of Antioch for making him look stupid, right? That's what that recording said, too. *Beheaded*. The end."

"Maybe he's the guy Margaret spurned instead. The one who had her eaten by the Dragon in the first place." Bess watched the gun in Greg's hand get lower and lower as they talked. Its barrel pointed somewhere around her navel.

"No, Bess. It's the Dragon. That man is long dead. But dragons are the kinds of things that can live forever."

"Or, I mean, not at all. Since they're imaginary." The gun raised back up a few inches and Bess cursed her own mouth for never knowing when to stop.

"Did it occur to you that maybe I'm doing the same thing you are? Looking for Amy?"

"It didn't," Bess said, honestly.

The radio behind her began to squawk and beep.

"Of course it didn't. Women are all alike. You don't want to give anyone the benefit of the doubt."

"Who doesn't?" Bess asked.

The radio went silent for a split second, then a steady hiss of static filled the room. But it wasn't empty static. There was something in there, swirling around.

ANTIOCH

"What's happening with that thing?" Greg motioned to the radio with the gun.

"It's picking something up. Greg, if you didn't hurt Amy, then tell me who did. Tell me what you know. If you're doing the same thing I am, then let's figure this out together."

Greg wasn't paying attention to her anymore. His eyes were on the radio as if it had transformed into something obscene. The static quieted, smoothed out like chaos morphing into jazz—a magic eye picture suddenly making itself visible.

This is Amy Eckhardt

The color drained from Greg's face. Bess reached forward and gently pulled the gun from his hand. He seemed not to notice.

This is Amy Eckhardt
It's going to happen
They're too close now
He's been sharpening his knives

"Shut the fuck up," Greg whispered without conviction.

He can't keep me anymore

"What the fuck is this? How are you doing this?" Greg demanded, looking at Bess.

"It's not me."

"I want to talk to her. How do I do that?"

"You don't. It doesn't work like that."

"The fuck you mean it doesn't work like that? Just . . . how do I talk to her?"

"I'm telling you, you can't talk to her any more than you can talk to fucking Taylor Swift on the radio."

I'm in the dragon's stomach
He'll spit out my head as proof

"Amy is dead," he shouted. "This is some god damned trick!"

The radio died as if an invisible hand had clicked it off.

Greg was shaking his head slowly back and forth. His lips were moving, but there were no sounds. He looked down at the hand that had once contained a gun and, finding it empty, simply walked out of the garage. Bess heard her front door open and then close as he left.

Bess set the gun down next to the radio and drifted into the main house. She locked the door and grabbed her cell phone from the kitchen counter. She did a mental rundown of all the people she could call and the pros and cons of each one. The list was short and there weren't many pros. Finally she decided to call Detective Howland. Even if he was a crooked cop, he was still a cop. And maybe that didn't mean anything at all, but Bess didn't have much else. Somewhere in all this there was a lesson about letting people into her life and it was a little too on the nose for her at the moment.

When she met Scott Howland at the door she glanced over at Rebecca's house, wondering if she was in there taking note of the cop car and fretting over her problem neighbor.

ANTIOCH

"I'm sorry to bother you, Detective," she said as she let him inside.

"It's Scott, remember? And it's not a bother. You did the right thing." He smiled at her and Bess told herself not to trust it.

"The gun's in here." She led the way to the garage and pointed, all business.

"Was Mr. Leeds wearing gloves when he touched it?"

"No, but neither was I. Both of our prints will be on it."

"That's fine. With any luck it'll be registered in his name. We've already got a BOLO out on him. We can't have men going around harassing women in Antioch. That sort of thing doesn't fly."

"Will you let me know if you find him? I'll feel safer knowing he's off the streets."

"Absolutely. I can also put a car outside if it'll make you feel better."

"I'd rather not, if that's okay. I don't think my neighbors would like it."

"Well, it would be for their protection as well."

"I don't know if they'd see it that way." Bess had tried so hard to stay out of trouble, to go unnoticed, and within a matter of days she'd managed to undo it all.

"Okay, no problem. No cops. Make sure you keep the doors locked. And call me if anything hinky happens."

You don't even know hinky, she thought.

She nodded. Scott pulled a large plastic evidence bag from his jacket and slid the gun carefully inside. "You know, I heard the funniest thing this morning. You won't believe it," he said, his voice casual.

"Try me," Bess said, nervous.

"I heard that you were having coffee yesterday with Cherish McKenzie." His smile didn't falter, but it seemed to change—maybe something in the eyes.

"Where would you hear something like that?"

"It's a small town, Bess. And I'm the eyes and ears of it. When someone whispers a secret in Antioch, I make it my business to hear it."

"So what? Yeah. Okay. I had coffee with Cherish yesterday. Why, do you know her or something?"

"Did she not mention me? Gosh, I'm a little hurt. Well, you see, Cherish and I used to be somewhat of an item. That's what they say, right? We were a thing. We were involved."

"It didn't come up."

"Well, what *did* come up?"

"Why do you want to know?"

"I'm curious what good old Cherish is up to these days. You know she's a drug addict, right?" The smile was still in place.

"I barely know her."

"She's a pill popper. It's why we broke up, if you want to know the truth. It made her paranoid. The thing about that is, after a while, even though you know what they're saying is nuts, if you hear it enough, it starts to sort of make sense. Especially if it's someone you love. Or something you want to believe."

He had an answer for everything. The man was standing in front of her building a case against a woman based on a conversation he'd not heard and it made perfect sense. Except Bess had seen too much to let him gaslight her.

"Well, she didn't have any crazy stories for me. Just a nice talk. About church," Bess said.

"I didn't know you were religious," Scott said. "I'm a little surprised."

"I haven't been to church in a long time. But this guy I work with, Wayne, he recommended First Baptist because of their young adult ministry. Cherish goes there."

"No, she doesn't."

Bess paused. Hadn't Cherish said she attended? Or was it only Margot and her family? "She does now. She's new to it, like me."

"So, you've decided you need Jesus?"

"Yeah. Keep me out of trouble. Isn't that what you want, Scott? For me to stay out of trouble?" She smiled at him.

"I want you to be safe."

"And what could be safer than a church?"

He considered this for a moment. "You know, part of me thought maybe you were talking to Cherish because you were checking up on me."

His candor caught her off guard, she sputtered a few syllables before giving up and shaking her head.

"That sounds crazy, doesn't it?" he asked. "We don't really know each other. But I can't help but feel like there's something between us. Do you feel like that?"

Bess felt the familiar heat rising to her face. "I hope I haven't given you the wrong impression." She peeked up at him from beneath her thick lashes and silently hoped she was giving the impression that she wanted him to fuck her.

He stepped toward her and laid his hand on her

upper arm. "I don't think you have." His hand slid up to her shoulder and then her throat. His thumb gently stroked her cheek and Bess shuddered. She turned her face in toward his palm and let his fingers trace her bottom lip. She closed her eyes and sighed.

"Scott," she said. His hands were on her hips now and he pulled her against him. She pressed into him and he let out a low groan of pleasure.

Bess knew she shouldn't be doing this. In fact, it was the worst idea possible, outside of, perhaps, Bible study with a serial killer. Reluctantly, she stepped back. Scott was still holding her hips and she felt them sway toward him, drawn back like a magnet. "I'm sorry," she said. "This isn't right." She regretted it immediately.

Scott's face regrouped and within seconds he was all business again. "Not a problem, Bess. I'm the one who should be sorry. That was unprofessional. Won't happen again." He picked up the evidence bag containing Greg's gun and ambled over to the front door. "I'll let you know if we find Greg. *When* we find Greg. It was nice seeing you again." He nodded, dipping his chin ever so slightly as a goodbye and let himself out.

Bess locked the door behind him. The house seemed terribly quiet. She tried not to linger on the fact that she could be fucking Scott Howland at that exact moment and instead focused on her next move. She would go to Bible study that night—for the first time since she was twelve years old.

12

THE FIRST BAPTIST CHURCH of Antioch was housed in a large red brick building. The stained-glass windows that lined the sides of the sanctuary were easily two stories tall and a mix of greens and whites. White stone steps led up to large white pillars and a row of ornately carved wooden doors.

But Bess wasn't going in through the main entrance that night. She'd called Wayne about the Bible study and he directed her to enter through a smaller, less grand building behind the main church. This building housed the Sunday school classrooms, a large fellowship hall, and what looked to be some sort of small auditorium. Bible study was in one of the larger Sunday school rooms toward the back of the building. There were little signs printed on copy paper leading the way.

Bess poked her head in and surveyed the soft sage green walls of the room. There were about ten people inside, most of them looked younger and it occurred

161

to her for the first time that "young adult" probably meant eighteen to twenty-five, and at thirty-five, she was more than stretching the definition. A man close to the doorway caught her eye and smiled.

"Excuse me," she said, returning the smile. "Is this the young adult Bible study?"

"It sure is," he said enthusiastically. "I'm Andy." He extended a hand and Bess shook it.

"Hi, I'm Bess. My friend Wayne recommended the group. Although, I might be a little old. Wayne knows my father and, you know, I think he still thinks of me as a kid."

"Nonsense, everyone's welcome here. And besides, you don't look very old to me."

Bess considered briefly if maybe Andy was hitting on her, but she quickly dismissed the idea. He seemed too wide open and pure to ever hit on a woman. "Well, I appreciate the compliment, Andy."

A circle of metal folding chairs sat in the center of the room and a couple of long faux wood finished tables pushed back against the walls and housed a coffee pot and a box of donuts. Bess smiled and made her way over to the coffee. She poured some into one of the disposable cups stacked next to the pot and smiled down at the beautiful caffeinated cup of something to do with her hands.

"Feel free to take a donut, too," Andy said. He'd followed her over to the table. "They're for everyone and we always have leftovers. And I end up taking them home and . . . " He patted his small belly to show where they would end up.

Bess gave him a small laugh. "I might have one after. But I'm grateful for the coffee." The cream was in a small silver pitcher and Bess spilled some into her cup. "Have you been coming here long?"

"Only my whole life," he said, smiling even more. "My folks go here and all that. How about yours?"

"Oh no, my family is Methodist. But I sort of got out of the habit and, you know, I thought I'd try my own thing."

"I think that's great. You'll like it here. Daniel's pretty great. He's intense sometimes. But he has these ideas, like, wow. Stuff you'd never think of on your own, you know? He has a lot of insight."

"He's the group leader?" Bess asked.

"Yep, you got it. In fact, he's already here. I can introduce you before we get started."

"Oh, oh man. I'm not—I don't want to be a bother." Bess nearly choked on the coffee she hadn't had a drink of yet. It was all happening faster than she'd anticipated. She'd hoped to stay back in the shadows and go unnoticed. Instead she'd run into Andy, the friendliest man alive, and now she was going to have a conversation with a man she believed could be a serial killer.

"It's no bother at all, he'll want to say hi. He always wants to meet new people." Andy stood on his tiptoes and waved to another man leaning against the opposite wall and having a conversation with a tall brunette woman in jeans and an oversized royal blue tee shirt with Cookie Monster's face on the front. "Brother Daniel, we have a visitor," Andy called. The man waved back at Andy and politely excused himself from the woman and approached them.

Daniel Mills was not a small man. In fact, Bess figured he was easily six foot three, possibly taller, yet he somehow didn't take up much space. He had an average build. Not remarkable. If she saw him on the street she would likely never notice him, or forget she'd seen him within seconds. He had dark hair and eyes and the flawless white skin of an actor. He grinned at her without showing any teeth and she was suddenly reminded of Anthony Perkins. She tried to push the image out of her mind, but the resemblance was uncanny. His face was a blank slate except for the wheels turning behind his eyes.

"Hi there," Daniel said. "It's nice to have you here."

Bess smiled and said nothing.

Daniel smiled at Andy, his eyes amused, wordlessly asking what the new girl's problem was.

"Okay, well, I'm glad to meet you," he continued. "We'll be getting started here in a few minutes, so make yourself at home."

"Thank you," Bess muttered. "Sorry, I just . . . " She drank some of her coffee, pretending it wasn't too hot. "Dry throat."

"Sure, of course. I'm Brother Daniel. I see you've already met Brother Andy. He's our unofficial welcome wagon. No one makes you feel welcome like Andy."

"He's been great, yeah. Uh, my name's Bess."

"Bess." Daniel said the name like she was an old friend he was embarrassed to have forgotten. "I think you'll enjoy this one, Bess." He turned his back to her and faced the center of the room. "Hey guys, why don't we get started here. We have a new member with us tonight, so let's make sure and show Bess some hospitality."

The small groups broke apart and took seats in the

circle of chairs. Bess watched Daniel sit and purposely sat as far from him as possible. There was a recognition in his face that made her uneasy. She told herself she was paranoid, that she was imagining things. Andy sat next to her and she felt grateful for his friendly aura.

"So last week we really dug into the story of Jesus in the desert," Daniel began. "This week I'd like to take some of those same themes and go in a different direction with it."

The group murmured happy agreements.

"This week we're going to focus on a different character from that story. We're going to focus on the Devil."

Bess drank from her coffee cup and noticed her hands were trembling slightly. The faces in the room were wide open and unafraid. They smiled, excited for what was to come.

Daniel continued. "We all know there are two sides to every story. That's the story of the universe. Good and Evil are just two sides of the same coin. You can't have one without the other. Without Good there is no Evil, and without witnessing evil, how would we ever truly know good? They exist in a balance." There were a few thoughtful nods. "Good and Evil exists in all of us. And it exists there equally. If God is always watching you, then I tell you so is the Devil."

"I thought that was Santa Claus that always watched us." Bess was surprised by her own voice. All eyes fell upon her.

"We have a participator here," Daniel said. "Good, wonderful. I like that. And yeah, Santa Claus, God, Satan, it's really all the same."

"If they're so equal, why does God always win?" Bess asked.

Daniel laughed. "Win? What, you mean in here?" He held up his Bible and waved it next to his head. "In this book, why does the Devil always lose? Hmm. I wonder." He smiled and cut his eyes around the room. The other people in the group giggled. "You see, you have to consider the source. What we have here, my friends, is an unreliable narrator." Daniel thumped the Bible on his leg and the room filled with laughter like Bess had walked into the middle of a good inside joke. "You all know what I'm saying. This is a narrator with an agenda. He keeps us so close to his narrative that we can't see beyond it, we can't see that there's more to the story. Two sides.

"For every life God saves, the Devil claims one for himself. And we know it's true. We know it is. Look at this world. Does Good always win? We say it's all part of the plan, but what if that plan is balance? What if the point of all this pain and suffering is to keep all the joy and happiness in check?

"The Devil is eternal and eternity has one hell of a long memory. What eluded him once will not elude him again. When Jesus drives a demon from one man, his great-great-great-great-grandchildren may one day wake up with that very demon tormenting them. And now we call it something like DNA or heredity. Alcoholism runs in his family. Violence. Mental illness. We must always remember, maybe God won a battle, but never the war."

The room was quiet now, no more inside jokes. She could see it all over their faces—the demons they all thought they harbored. The suffering they endured. Daniel's words sunk down around them like a weight.

"We see it right here in Antioch!" he said. "The Devil is winning now, isn't he? Oh yes, the Devil is winning. Those women . . . six women, lost to the Devil right here in our own town. And can we say it was God that murdered them? No, God did not win on that day."

He looked at Bess, his eyebrow cocked, asking if she had any questions. If she wanted to add anything else to his lesson.

After a long pause he smiled again and took a deep breath. "Okay, so let's get into the scripture. We're going to be reading from the Book of Revelation, chapter twelve, starting with verse seven. 'Then war broke out in heaven; Michael and his angels battled against the dragon. The dragon and its angels fought back, but they did not prevail and there was no longer any place for them in heaven. The huge dragon, the ancient serpent, who is called the Devil and Satan, who deceived the whole world, was thrown down to earth, and its angels were thrown down with it.'"

Bess let the words settle down over her. The Dragon. He was playing with her. Her eyes were riveted to his face as he spoke.

"That's a lot, isn't it?" he asked the room. A few people nodded in agreement. "The Dragon is thrown down to earth. That sounds like a win, doesn't it, Bess? That's the win we expect. But then it goes on, doesn't it? If we keep reading, let's see, here at verse seventeen, 'Then the dragon became angry with the woman and went off to wage war against the rest of her offspring, those who keep God's commandments and bear witness to Jesus.' The story tells us of a woman. And God protects this woman. The whole earth rises up and protects this one woman. So to her way of thinking, yeah, God must have won. But that's not the end of the story. He may have missed that woman, but the Devil's going to wage war on her offspring. She may have evaded him once, but she can't forever."

After the lesson, Bess stayed behind, refilling her coffee cup and taking one of the donuts at Andy's insistence. Daniel came over and filled a cup for himself.

"I don't normally drink coffee so late. It keeps me up," he said, his voice pleasant and even.

"I don't sleep much either way," Bess said.

"So, what did you think?"

"It was different. I don't think I've ever heard a sermon that glorified the Devil quite like that."

He laughed. "Glorified? Me? No, it's not like that. We're realists here."

"And what's real?"

"The Devil. The Devil *is* real, Bess. And the little stories they tell us in the Bible are only the half of it. Some old men decided these are the stories we should know, but there's so much more. So many other perspectives. I want these guys to see that. To understand."

"What's that? You want them to understand that sometimes the Devil wins?"

"About half the time." He grinned, another joke. "But come on, think about it. The Devil put one over on us a long time ago and everybody's still living in the dark."

"What do you mean?"

"Jesus. The Son of God. I mean, come on. It doesn't really make any sense."

"You mean you think he was just a man? Some kind of con man that duped us? That's not something I expect to hear from a Bible study leader."

"No, you misunderstand me. You see, scholars pretty much agree these days, Mary, the Mother of Jesus, was probably raped by Roman soldiers. Immaculate? Not so much. She was a thirteen-year-old girl who got raped. And in those days she'd be stoned for something like that. So to save her life, they came up with a story. And it's, well, it's *quite* a story. I mean, it's a doozy. But riddle me this, Bess . . . Does a horrible rape sound like the way God would bring his son into the world? Or does that sound more like the way demons are spawned?" Daniel's eyes were far away, seeing something beyond the walls of the church.

"What are you even implying? That Jesus is the Devil?"

"Not at all. No. That's not how these things work. And I'd never say that. But the antichrist we've come to fear, what if he already came? What if he came and tricked us all?"

"That's ridiculous. Jesus preached about love." Bess was becoming frustrated. She wasn't sure she even believed in God, but here she was defending the ideals of Christianity.

"Maybe he did. But how many wars have been fought in his name? How many murders? I think Jesus's name has inspired more death and destruction than the Devil's."

"The Devil is a liar."

"Or is he a realist?" Daniel sipped his coffee.

"You weren't raised around here, were you?"

"No." Daniel's grin widened. "No, I wasn't raised in Antioch. I was raised . . . somewhere else."

"Did you know Margot Cooper? You had to have. She attended here, didn't she?" The question jumped from Bess's mouth before she could stop it. It hung there, an accusation.

"I knew Margot as she was. I do not know her anymore." Daniel's face looked different suddenly. It was less assured and confident, even his clean and even skin tone seemed to grey slightly, look oilier than before.

"Is that a yes?" Bess asked.

"Of course I knew her."

"It's awful what happened to her," Bess said, her eyes locked on his face.

"It was awful," he agreed, "at first. It's gotten easier over time."

And then Andy was beside them, nudging his way in between. "Looks like you two have become besties already! And Bess was worried she wouldn't fit in." He gave her a conspiratorial wink.

"I'd say she fits right in," Daniel said, regaining his composure.

The change in his appearance had been brief, but Bess was shaken by it. Talking about Margot had brought something out in him. Something smaller and weaker.

"I'd love to stay and talk more, but I really have to be getting home. Things to tend to. You know how it is." He eased out of the room, smiling to people as he passed. Once he was gone, everyone else seemed to take it as their cue to go as well.

Bess wasn't interested in walking to her car alone, so she waved goodbye to Andy and attached herself to a small group of women headed for the parking lot together. The inside of her car was muggy. She turned the air on and let it blow full blast for a minute before putting the car into gear and pulling away from the church.

Detective Howland's car was in front of her house when she arrived. He hopped out of the vehicle as soon as she was parked and met her in the middle of the lawn.

"Where have you been?" he asked.

"I told you earlier I was going to church. Why are you here? I said I didn't want any cops hanging around the place."

"I'm not here as a cop. I've been thinking about earlier and, well, I feel a little guilty. I hope I didn't come across like I was pressuring you in any way. It was unprofessional. I shouldn't have done it."

"You didn't. It's fine, Scott." Bess allowed herself to relax a little. Here in her front yard, surrounded by houses and families, she felt almost normal. "I don't really date much, to be honest. And under the circumstances, well, it seems . . . I don't know the word."

"It's bad timing."

"Yes, exactly. It's bad timing."

"And you don't trust me."

171

JESSICA LEONARD

Bess blinked. She was apparently too easy to read because everyone knew her at a glance. "I don't." She was tired of lying and keeping secrets.

"Is it because I don't want you investigating a series of murders?"

"It's because you either don't believe me about the things I've told you or you're choosing not to believe me. I can't shake the idea that you want Tam to be guilty, even if he isn't."

"Ouch." Scott scratched his chin and turned his eyes to the sky above her head. "It's not that you don't trust me. You think I'm an altogether piece of shit."

"I don't even know you."

"That's fair. I don't know you either. Which is probably why I'm not taking your intuition, or whatever you want to call it, as gospel." He looked back into her eyes and Bess noted that the kindness was gone from them. She'd hit him where it hurt, right in the career. "I'm good at my job, Miss Jackson."

"I thought we'd graduated to first names."

"Maybe that was premature."

"I hear you. It was nice of you to stop by, Detective. I'll be sure to call you if any crazy killers break into my house or anything." Bess turned away, not waiting for a response, and walked inside the house.

She peered out the front window as Scott's car pulled away from the curb. He hadn't wasted any time looking longingly back at her. She retrieved a beer from the refrigerator. She opened it with her tulip bottle opener and winced at the cold as it traveled down her throat.

172

ANTIOCH

She didn't have time for Scott Howland.

She thought back to what Daniel Mills had told her after Bible study had ended. She let her imagination follow the breadcrumbs he'd laid out for her. Jesus Antichrist carefully setting up a religion full of zealots brought in by Paul the False Prophet. Martyring himself to ensure his legacy. The Dragon sitting back, relaxing as the world burns.

But it was all a distraction. She could lose herself for hours in the possibilities. And Mills knew it. He'd shown himself early on, and maybe he regretted it. The thought excited her. She was close to something, closer than he liked. The key was in the lesson, not the lines he fed her after. The Dragon was making up for what eluded him in the past. Saint Margaret may have crawled from his mouth, but poor Margot hadn't been so lucky.

Bess finished her beer and padded out to the garage. Amy didn't have much time left—maybe it had already run out. She turned on the radio, let the static settle over her and contemplated her next move. She needed proof, undeniable proof the police couldn't ignore or sweep under the rug.

The static changed to a buzz and then a shrill whine. Bess winced and put her hands to her ears, muffling the noise.

SOS
SOS
My name is Amelia Earhart

Bess shook her head to clear away the false information.

JESSICA LEONARD

This is Amelia Earhart

"The fuck . . . " She wasn't misunderstanding this time. The woman on the transmission was saying Amelia Earhart.

Help me
Waters high
SOS
Help us quick
I can feel it
New York City
New York City
New York City
Oh, if they could hear me

Bess's stomach turned over. The room spun around her, slowly at first then gaining momentum. She knew exactly what she was hearing. It was the supposed final message of Amelia Earhart, stranded on Gardner Island, desperate for help. She'd read those words a thousand times, she knew them by heart.

George
Get the suitcase in my closet
SOS
Will you help me
Will you please
New York
New York

ANTIOCH

The transmission cut out there. Static swelled back up and claimed the garage. Bess could barely breathe. Her hands shook. The voice still echoed in her mind. Amelia Earhart. Her life's greatest obsession. The heroine and mystery she adored above all others. Tears first welled in her eyes and tumbled down her cheeks. Amelia Earhart.

A low, hollow monotone rose up and replaced the static.

Act One. Margaret of Antioch spurns the advances of Olybrius.
Act Two. Margaret of Antioch is tortured.
Act Three. Margaret of Antioch is swallowed by a dragon.
Act Four. Saint Margaret of Antioch is disgorged by the dragon.
Act Five. Saint Margaret of Antioch is beheaded.
MARGARET!

The voice screeched across Bess's mind like nails on a chalkboard. The voice was pain and torment.

You be GOOD NOW, Margaret!

And then it changed once more. The shrill rage quieted and a deep calm replaced it. It resonated in her bones, unnaturally low and painfully masculine.

But you're not Margaret.

Her breath was coming in thin gasps. She felt like

she was being watched. Bess whipped around to look behind her. The garage door was closed. She was alone.

Not Margaret. Not chosen. Not Margot or Ashley. Not Brandy, Emily, Bethany, or Olivia. Not Amy. Just a girl. Not special. Not chosen.

"Who are you?" Bess cried.

You know who I am.
I see you, Bess Jackson.

"Tell me who you are!"

I am the Dragon. I live inside the weak, but they do my will because they want to.

"You're a psychopath and you kill people because you're crazy."

The world denies me until I am a harmless fairy tale.
And then I rise.

"You're a sick man with a god complex. No matter how much you think you've changed, you're still only yourself."

You only make me stronger.
I see you now, Bess Jackson.
And you have done my will.

ANTIOCH

*Yes, I can see you
Because it was also your will.*

"No," Bess screamed. "The Devil is a liar."

God is the liar. I only show you the truest truth—the truth you're scared to admit to yourself. The truth that haunts you in nightmares and gnaws at your heart.

"Shut up."

All these disappearances. People leaving town. What's one more—right, Bess Jackson?

"Shut up."

I see you.

"Stop it." Tears coursed down Bess's cheeks.

*Where did your fiancé Brandon end up, Bess Jackson?
Yes, I see you
I see you
I see you
I see you
I see you*

Bess acted without thinking. In one smooth motion she knocked her radio to the floor and stomped down hard with her boot. And everything went silent. The crunch was oddly anticlimactic. Her most prized possession, trash on her floor. She was alone now, cut off.

Just like Amelia.
Just like Amy.

13

SOMEWHERE NEAR THE river there was a house with a basement and Bess was going to find it. Daniel Mills's address was easy enough to locate with a quick Google search. He lived on Poplar, only a few blocks from Greg Leeds. He might not be keeping Amy there, but it was at least a place to start.

She rushed to her bedroom and changed into a pair of black yoga pants and an oversized, charcoal grey hoodie. She wanted to be covert. It felt like a game, but without any rules or possibility of winning.

It was cooler after the sun set, but still much too warm to be wearing a sweatshirt. Bess pretended not to care as she casually walked down Aviary Street, glancing at the foundations of homes and businesses as she passed. Dead trees, like gnarled arthritic fingers, clawed up from the bank of the Reddington River. Barges slid noiselessly downstream, their long black bodies opaque against the moonlit water. Only their absence of reflection gave them away out there.

Like a hole punched through reality into some other place where black spaces stole light and never gave it back.

Not a lot of basements along the river.

Bess turned down Poplar Street, which ran parallel to Aviary. In some towns, houses near the water would be nicer, more expensive—the land considered prime real estate. Antioch was not one of those towns. The homes here ranged from decent to ramshackle with most in the in-between area Bess would describe as "rundown."

Two blocks down and Bess was already beginning to feel frustrated. She'd seen two homes with basement windows instead of vented crawlspaces, but after poking around she decided both were harmless. Her cell phone was snug in the kangaroo pocket of her hoodie and she kept her hands on it as she walked, reminding herself it wasn't lost and that help was only a call away if she needed it. She wasn't sure Scott Howland would be eager to answer her calls, but she hoped.

The address for Daniel Mills was still two blocks down. Bess stopped at what appeared to be an old storefront building. The windows were boarded up. Above the door a sign hung slightly askew on time-loosened nails. The paint had faded and worn down to the bare wood in some spots, but large red letters at the center still declared "VHS". Bess thought she noticed the tell-tale small rectangular windows along the bottom of the structure. Trying to seem as if she belonged there, Bess left the sidewalk and veered into the little gravel lot of the old store. There was definitely a basement, soft yellow light bled out from one of those windows. She eased along the side of the structure and knelt beside the window, but it was too grimy to see anything inside.

Bess stood and slowly crept to the front of the building, but the shrill whine of rusted hinges made her stop short. Someone was coming out of the building's front door. Bess pressed her body flat against the side of the wall and held her breath, watching. A man stepped out onto the sidewalk and paused under the streetlight, looking back. At first, Bess wasn't sure if it was Greg, or if she just wanted it to be, in the way your brain makes you see faces in inanimate objects because it wants things to make sense, to be easy. The way you hear words like Bevington instead of Reddington or New York City instead of Norwich City. But there was no reasoning it away. That was Greg Leeds. He headed north along Poplar and Bess counted to ten before inching her way out of hiding and onto the street. He was already out of sight, probably turning on a side street to take him back home to Aviary.

For a few seconds she stood there, trying to decide if she should call Detective Howland. But what would she say? Greg Leeds came out of a building? It wasn't the most damning evidence, and she needed something concrete. Bess followed Greg away from Daniel's house.

She was trying to keep her breathing as quiet as possible when a hand clapped over her mouth. Her startled shriek died behind a man's pressing palm.

"What's this?" Greg whispered into her ear. "A concerned citizen out for a midnight stroll?" His other hand snaked around her middle, pulling her body in close to his own. She could smell stale sweat, old cigarettes, and something else—the high metallic scent of adrenaline pumping through a scared animal.

"You're starting to become a real nuisance, Bess. There's been cops driving around here all day."

Bess bit into Greg's hand and kicked backward with all her strength, hoping to connect with something soft and vital. He cried out and his grip relaxed out of instinct. Bess threw an elbow back against the bony middle of his chest. Loose gravel scrunched under her sneakers as she ran. Bess yanked her cell phone from her pocket and dialed 911 without slowing down. No time to hope for Howland. She needed someone immediately.

"My name is Bess Jackson." The words came out in bursts, punctuated by hard desperate breaths. "I'm on Poplar Street near the river. A man just attacked me. He's chasing me. I need help."

"I've dispatched police to your area. Do you know who attacked you?"

Bess's lungs burned as she struggled to respond. "His name's Greg Leeds. White man, six foot, slender."

"Ma'am? I can barely understand you. What's happening?"

She considered slowing down or stopping, but only for a split second. That was how people died.

Bess ran until blue lights flashed behind her and a loud voice told her to stop. She raised her hands and yelled back that she was Bess Jackson, that she had called the police. She lay on the pavement when they told her to. She placed her hands on the back of her head. She stayed still and quiet. A police dog sniffed at her body. She was told to get on her knees and then her feet. She was patted down, and finally taken to the station to give a statement.

"What in the fuck were you doing stalking Greg Leeds?" Scott Howland asked, exasperated.

"I wasn't stalking him. I wasn't looking for him at all. I was looking for . . . houses with basements."

"Thinking of moving?"

Bess stared into his eyes until he shifted uncomfortably in his seat. "Greg jumped me. Right out there on the street. He was coming out of that old video store on Poplar. You have to check it out."

"Well, someone owns that old building, believe it or not, so we can't just bust down the doors."

"Isn't this probable cause? I'm sure I've heard that phrase before."

"You know what happens to illegally obtained evidence? It gets thrown out in court. It loses cases. If you're up to something, I'm begging you to tell me what it is."

"I'm not up to anything."

"Whoever told you I'm your enemy . . . how do you know they're your friend? How can you be so sure you're looking at this through the right perspective?"

Bess remembered Daniel talking about Jesus. Just because you're told someone is good or bad or holy or maybe pure evil, that doesn't make it so. She'd spent her teens and twenties looking critically at religion and faith and deciding things for herself. It was a disservice to who she was to throw all that away now. She needed to choose for herself who her allies would be.

"Do you know a man named Daniel Mills?" Bess asked.

Scott sighed. He'd been pacing the room, but it was as if he was suddenly too tired to keep it up and he sank down into the chair opposite Bess. He closed his eyes and rubbed the bridge of his nose. "Daniel the Baptist," he said.

"It's him, Scott. I know it is. He killed those women and he's got Amy."

"Slow down. Now I'll admit, we looked at Mills way back when Margot Cooper disappeared, but it didn't work out. The math didn't work."

"But maybe your math was flawed."

"You're talking about the time of death and all that? God, you are deep in the conspiracy theories."

"They're my life," Bess said.

"It's true, there could be some issues with our timeline. But what about all the other women? Do you know all those timelines? Does he fit all of them? You've been on this case for a couple weeks. There's no way you have all the details worked out."

"I don't. But Tam Gillis did."

"And of course you've been talking to Tam."

"Scott, I have something to show you. But if I do, I want you to promise me you won't use it in court or anything like that."

"I absolutely cannot make that promise."

They looked at each other, neither willing to budge.

"You want me to trust you," said Bess. "Well, I need you to trust me too. Fuck. Okay. I can compromise. Come to my house. Let me show you the proof about Daniel Mills and then, if you don't believe me, you forget what I said and move along."

"That's exactly what you want. It's in no way a

compromise," he said, but he was smiling, and Bess knew she had him.

"You owe me this."

"How? You know what, forget it. Fine. The fact is, if you have evidence, I need to see it. Show me what you've got and we'll go from there."

Scott Howland sat on Bess's couch waiting impatiently as she dug through Tam's notes for the specifics on Daniel Mills.

"Just show me everything," he called to her.

"I'll only be a minute," she called back. She had no intention of letting Scott see the stalker notebooks, only the ones specifically pertaining to Mills and his whereabouts and connections to the victims.

She came into the room with an armload of notes and two beers resting gently on the top of the stack. "I know it's not professional," she said. "And shit, I guess I don't even know if you drink, but I thought . . . "

"I'd love a beer. I feel like I've earned it at this point. We'll consider this some off-duty research." He stood up, took the drinks from the top of the stack and opened them.

"Off duty is exactly what I'm looking for." Bess pulled the notebook labeled "Daniel Mills" from the pile and opened it. "Okay, so the stuff about Margot you mostly know," she said, pointing to the timelines neatly detailed on the first few pages. "He could have easily kidnapped her and left the head if you look at the longest possible timeframe."

"Sure, I'll give you that one. And he knew her. They were members of the same church. There was some . . . infatuation on his part, right?" he asked.

"Right."

"So, what's the connection to Ashley Bunkirk? Tell me how this works."

"Ashley worked at the movie theater. Daniel Mills goes to that theater almost every week. He would have had to have seen her there."

"I go to the movies too, am I a suspect?"

"Don't be an asshole. He also has no alibi for the times when she disappeared and when her head was found. And maybe you think that's a coincidence. But what if I said she was at Mills's Bible study group the week before she disappeared?"

"That's a little more. What about the others?"

"I'll save you the suspense and tell you he has no alibi for any of the victims," Bess said. "He knew them all. They didn't all go to Bible study. That would be too easy. And he's too smart to get all his victims from his own class. Too suspicious."

"Sure, that makes sense." Scott nodded.

"He works at Lowe's in lawn and garden. Olivia Terry was in the middle of building a deck when she disappeared. Bethany Ladd was the office manager at STL Construction, they bought most of their raw materials from Lowe's and Bethany managed every purchase order and pickup." Bess paused long enough to have a few swallows of beer. The more she talked, the more excited she became. She'd done the right thing, bringing Scott here. There was no way he'd be able to deny all of these as coincidences. "Emily and Brandy are a little more random. He and Brandy both ate lunch at the café pretty regularly, which I know doesn't sound like much. Emily, I'm not sure he knew at all. But her disappearance is what stands out. She was a jogger and she'd apparently gone for a run by the river. That's what her boyfriend said. And Daniel lives by the river."

Scott was quiet for a few minutes. He squinted at the notebook in front of him. "Bess, I can't help but think if we picked anyone in town at random, we'd be able to make similar connections. They're not enough for a search warrant, let alone an arrest."

Bess's heart fell. She'd been so certain he'd want to help. She drank to mask her frustration. "Well, I'm happy you could come by. You can go ahead and leave."

"God damn, Bess. Don't be that way. I'm here to help you."

She rolled her eyes and went for another beer.

"I am, I promise. But I have to work within the law. You have to understand, without more I can't do anything as a detective."

"What good are detectives?" she cried. "Fuck, do you even detect? Have you tried even some minor sleuth work?"

"What do you want me to do?"

"Try! I met this guy and I can tell you he isn't right. Not at all. Interview some people. At least talk to the guy, can't you do that? Talk?"

He sighed and ran his hand through his hair. "Okay, I can talk to him. Will that make you happy?"

"It's a start."

"And what about Greg Leeds? How's he connected to this?"

"There's another notebook on Greg." Bess flipped through the stack of notes on her coffee table and brought out the journal with Greg's information in it.

Howland took the book and turned it over in his hand. "This one's fancy."

"Yeah, I noticed that," Bess said.

"Even the handwriting is different."

"Maybe Winnie Tate made that one," Bess suggested, forgetting momentarily that she was supposed to be keeping her source a secret.

He shook his head and thumbed through the book. "There aren't any correlations here. No connections between this one and the other notes, not with the victims or Daniel Mills."

"I don't know, maybe they decided he wasn't a suspect. All I know is, something about Greg doesn't make sense. He's erratic. He . . . he knows something. I don't know what."

"So we'll keep looking for Greg and I'll bring in Mills for questioning. Can I keep the journal?" Scott asked.

"Of course, take all of it." Bess pointed to the notes.

"Thanks, just the Greg Leeds book for now."

"Thank you, Scott." She felt so much relief welling up inside her that she thought she might burst. She reached out her hand and placed it over his. "You don't know how much this means to me."

He smiled. "Do you mind if I grab another drink?"

"Help yourself. I'm going to hit the bathroom real quick."

Bess ambled back to the bathroom. Checking her reflection in the mirror, she wiped gently at the circles under her eyes. She looked tired. But hell, she *was* tired.

Scott wasn't on the couch when she came back into the living room. She noticed the garage door was ajar.

"What are you doing?" she asked.

"I wanted to see the radio. What the fuck happened?"

"Oh, it broke," she said, embarrassed.

"And everything else?"

"Everything what?" She glanced past him into the room.

"There's got to be thirty beer bottles in here, and it looks like there was some sort of fight . . . "

Broken glass bottles littered the edge of the wall. "I broke a few. You know, frustrated. Nothing . . . I mean this isn't . . . I guess it's a little bit messy." She felt irritated. Why was he even in here? What right did he have to criticize her housekeeping? "You know, let's get out of here. The radio broke. It's no big deal."

"Yeah, sure." Scott gave her a small smile. "I'm going to get out of here. I need to get some sleep. I have a lot of work to do tomorrow."

"Oh, yeah. Absolutely. I should get to bed too. Thank you again, Scott."

He left without another word and Bess was once again alone. The house seemed different. She suddenly felt intruded upon. The clock said it was pushing midnight. She should sleep. Things would make more sense in the morning.

14

CAROL WAS AT the front counter with Wayne when Bess came into work the next day. They were leaning in together. "Thick as thieves," Bess's mother had always said.

"What are you two conspiring about?" she asked.

"Not conspiring," Carol said. "We *were* talking about you, though."

"I should go put the new stock out," Wayne said, sliding out from behind the counter and around Carol. "I heard you were at Bible study the other night, Bess."

"I was, yeah, the people were really nice."

"They are. Real nice bunch. I'm glad you liked it. It's good for you. Can't have enough of that goodness in your life." He gave her a pat on the back on his way to the back room.

"So why are you talking about me?" Bess asked.

"You're basically the talk of the town," Carol said. "Do tell."

"Detective Howland was in here earlier. He was

ANTIOCH

looking at the journals we have for sale. Oh, and asking about you."

"About me? Are you sure?"

"Yeah, I'm pretty sure. He wanted to know how you'd been at work. If you were erratic lately. About your job performance."

"And what did you tell him?"

"I told him you were as terrible as usual," Carol deadpanned. "What do you think? I told him you're a model employee. Always on time. No personal issues. I basically lied, but shit, I care more about you than I do some stranger cop. But now I need to know what's happening."

"Nothing's happening," Bess said.

"Come on. You *are* acting a little erratic. I come over and your place is a wreck. There's mud on the windows, trash all over the place, and when was the last time you really slept? You've been looking more and more ragged every time I've seen you."

"I'm fine. Things have been a little off. I'm . . . I don't know. I'm going through some things." Bess felt tears rising and clenched her jaw to keep them at bay.

"I offered you time off if you needed it. The offer still stands."

"Let me work today. Carol, please. I need this." She didn't know why she needed it, but she did. She needed the normalcy of it, the routine. She needed to feel like a part of the world, like anyone else.

"Work today. But then you're taking a week off, and it's not negotiable." Carol was sterner than Bess had ever seen her. There was no place for argument.

Bess nodded. "You can go get something done, I'll cover the counter."

191

Carol left her there without another word. Bess imagined what life would be like if Carol fired her until the tears threatened to spill from her eyes and she had to distract herself by straightening the candy bars beneath the counter.

The front door swung open and Bess gave a bright, "Hello," without looking up.

"Hello to you too, Bess."

Bess's head moved so quickly her neck cried out in protest. Daniel Mills was only feet from her, and she quickly moved behind the counter in order to have something between them.

"What are you doing here?" she asked.

"Well, I came to see you, Bess. I thought that would be obvious." He was smiling at her and the sight of his teeth made her anxious.

"Why would you want to see me?"

"I very much enjoyed having you in my class. I wanted to invite you back. Any time." He sauntered up to the counter and leaned in toward her. Bess stepped backward, pressing herself against the wall. "You know," he continued, "it's funny how I had no idea about you. I mean, it's a small town. You'd think you'd know just about everybody. But here you were— a total stranger to me. Hiding."

Bess shook her head. "No."

"Not hiding, you say? No, maybe being hidden."

"Can I help you?" Wayne appeared, a stack of new releases in his hands. Bess had never been so happy to see him.

"No, thank you," Daniel said, turning toward him. "I was having a chat with our newest Bible study buddy!"

"Oh, Brother Daniel, I didn't recognize you," Wayne said, smiling. He juggled the weight of the books over to one arm and stuck out his right hand in order to shake Daniel's hand.

Daniel gave it an exaggerated pump. "Wayne Wilkes! It is so so good to see you. I hear we have you to thank for Bess coming in and visiting us."

"It's true," Wayne beamed. "I told her over and over she needed to get into that study group. Told her how much she'd like it."

"Well, I can't speak for her, but we sure liked having her."

The whole scene was too surreal, Bess felt the room tilt on its side and she gripped the counter hard to keep herself upright. Hot bile rose in her throat and she struggled to swallow it down.

"She loved it," Wayne said. "Of course she did."

"Of course," Daniel agreed.

Bess fainted.

Carol was standing over her when she awoke. Her face was drawn, and Bess could see every line in exaggerated detail. Bess felt clammy, her body covered in a cold sweat. She tried to sit up and Carol put a hand on her shoulder, gently keeping her where she was.

"Don't get up too quick," she said. "I never should have let you work today." This was more to herself, but it felt like a slap to Bess's face.

"I didn't mean to," Bess said, childlike in her weakened state.

"Of course not," Daniel said, crouching at her feet like a tiger.

"Thank God you're okay," Carol said

193

"Well, let's not give him the credit for everything," Daniel said.

"I'm sorry," Bess said. She sat up and rubbed her eyes.

Wayne slid down next to her and held out a plastic bottle of juice. "I ran down to the deli and got you some orange juice. For your sugar."

"Thank you, Wayne."

"You should go home," Carol told her.

"I don't mind driving her," Daniel volunteered.

"No," Bess cried out, startling everyone. Everyone except Daniel, who smiled. "I can drive."

"Absolutely not," Carol said.

"Then, can you call Detective Howland for me?"

"What? Is he your legal guardian now?"

"I need to talk to him, anyway."

"Sure, why the fuck not. He gave me his card earlier. I'll track it down." Carol got up and walked away.

"What happened?" Wayne asked.

"I have no idea," Bess answered. "I've never fainted before in my life."

"Well, if you're taken care of, I should probably be leaving," Daniel said, standing. "I don't want to be in the way when the good detective arrives. I've taken enough of his time."

"What do you mean?" Bess asked.

"He came and saw me at work today. Bright and early. Had a nice chat. But now I really must be going." Bess watched Daniel disappear out the front doors.

"Wayne, how long have you known Daniel?"

"Well, since he moved here, I guess. I don't know him well. But we do go to—"

"The same church, yeah, I remember. Does he seem . . . I don't know, strange to you?"

Wayne considered for a moment. "He seems less strange now than he used to, if you can believe that. When he first moved to town he seemed sickly."

"He was sick?"

"I don't think so, he just *seemed* it. He had real bad skin, never really looked clean. I hate to admit it, but people steered clear of him. But then in the last couple years he's turned around. Looks healthier. More confident."

"Last couple years? You mean literally, like two years?"

"Maybe. Two or three sounds right. Why do you ask?"

"I'm not sure. He makes me a little uncomfortable, to be honest." Wayne's face fell. "Don't take it personally. Everyone else at the church was very nice. Honestly. It's nothing against the place. He makes me feel nervous."

Wayne sighed. "I wish I could be more surprised. But if I'm being fair, he does me too. Something about that smile. Like he's waiting for his chance to bite."

"Exactly."

"Let's get you up outta this floor. Don't tell Carol, but I don't clean it as much as I should."

Wayne walked with her over to the bar where he hovered around her as she situated herself on a stool, ready to catch her if needed.

"The detective is on his way. He said he wanted to talk to you too, and I think this whole situation is fucked," Carol declared as she joined them. "I don't

195

know what your relationship is with this guy, but I don't fucking approve."

"I don't have a relationship, Carol. I promise you, I'm quite alone."

"I thought you were seeing that white boy," Wayne said.

"Greg? No, that . . . it didn't work out."

"Are you seeing this cop or what?" Carol asked.

"Not at all."

"Good, I wouldn't want to think your boyfriend was snooping around here asking about you. That doesn't seem healthy."

"Nope, just the perfectly normal healthy practice of a police detective snooping around asking about me."

"I should get back to work," Wayne said.

"You've got no flare for the dramatic, either," Carol said.

"I'm sorry for being dramatic," Bess said.

"Oh, stop it. I don't want you to be sorry. I want you to feel better and come back to work. Can you do that for me?"

"I'll try my best," Bess promised.

"Then we're good." Carol smiled for the first time since Bess had come to work. "Your handsome detective has arrived."

She motioned toward the door and Bess turned to see Scott Howland duck into the store. He caught her eye immediately and grinned before he could catch himself and arrange his features back into the hard non-expression of a professional.

"Carol told me you had a bit of a scare," he said.

"I fainted. Is that what you mean?"

"I guess it is. Should we go?"

"Thank you," Bess said. Carol handed her her purse and Bess followed Scott out to his car.

"They told me you were there today, asking about me," Bess said as soon as they were moving.

"It's my job."

"It's your job to ask my boss if I'm crazy? Am I suddenly a suspect?"

"You are not."

"Daniel Mills came into my store earlier and basically threatened me."

"Are you serious?" Scott asked. "What did he say to you?"

"What did *you* say to *him?* He told me you'd been there this morning. Apparently you're having an enormously busy day."

"I stopped by his work. Asked him a few questions. Which is what you wanted me to do, right?"

Bess didn't know why she was angry with Scott, but she was, stubbornly so, and she didn't know how to let it go. "I did. What did you talk about? What did he say?"

"I can't tell you that."

"Why?"

"Why do you think? It's police business and I swear to God, if I have to tell you one more time that you are not a detective I'm going to drive you down to the next town and leave you there. Let you be their problem. Now, did he or did he not threaten you? Tell me what he said."

"He . . . thanked me for coming to his Bible study."

"Yeah, that's basically what he said to me. He was

happy to have you in his class. You were very nice and enthusiastic," Scott said.

"You don't believe it's him, do you?"

"I don't know what to believe, Bess."

They arrived at Bess's home, but she made no move to get out of the car. "What do you mean?" she asked.

"I mean . . . nothing you've told me makes any sense. I want to believe it, but I can't."

"Well, fuck you, Detective." Bess jumped out of the car and slammed the door as hard as she could, nearly pulling herself off her feet as she did so.

Scott was out and on her heels before she even reached her front stoop. "Don't run off, I still need to talk to you and I'd rather do it here, but if you make me, I'll bring you into the station."

"Are you fucking kidding me? Daniel Mills gets to come by my job and walk the streets and what the fuck ever, and you're going to take me to the god damned police station?"

"Please let me come in. Let me talk to you without all the distractions and the attitude and bullshit."

Bess opened the front door and walked in, leaving it open behind her, a passive invitation. "What do you want to talk about?"

"Can we sit?"

Bess flopped down hard on the couch. "Sit."

Scott rolled his eyes and joined her.

"Look, if you don't want to believe me about Mills, then we need to find Greg. He knows more than I do. He's scared. But maybe he has a good reason to be. If you can find Greg, you'll have more than just my word," Bess said.

ANTIOCH

Scott ran a hand through his hair. He let out a small growl of frustration. "Stop with the Greg stuff. I don't get it, but it's not helping."

"What are you talking about? What isn't helping?"

"Greg. Greg Leeds. The mysterious man that no one knows."

"No one knows? *I* know him. He was Amy's *boyfriend*," Bess said. She felt the same cold sweat from earlier form across her brow and she swiped at it absently. Her head was spinning.

"Amy didn't have a boyfriend," Scott shouted.

"What is this? Of course she did. Her roommate called me and told me she did." The room had taken on an oddly blueish hue and Bess leaned back on the couch and closed her eyes.

"She called you?" Scott asked.

"I . . . I called her. But then, she called me back . . . ." She was confused, floundering.

"But you told me you already knew him." Scott had taken a small digital voice recorder out of his jacket pocket and showed it to Bess. "Do you mind if I record this?"

"Sure," Bess said. "Um, me and Greg dated. Not dated. Had one date."

"And where did you go on that date?"

"I . . . I can't remember." Bess rubbed her eyes.

"You can't remember a date? Must have been outstanding."

"What difference does it make? We went out. We went out. And then he came to my work."

"Did he talk to anyone there?" Scott asked. "Did anyone see him?"

"No. Everyone was . . . Lucy was in the back, I

think." Bess scrunched up her face and tried to remember.

"Then there's the address you gave me for him, on Aviary, it's no good." Scott stared at his hands.

"I was there. You found me there on the street. You basically tackled me while I was running away from him."

"I saw you on the street running like a mad woman. There was no one else there."

"I am not mad," Bess said.

"There's no one on that street with the name Leeds. Or even Greg," Scott said.

"Maybe . . . it's in Amy's name?" Bess leaned forward, elbows on knees, face in hands. "Stop this," she muttered. "Please, I don't feel well. Maybe I've misremembered. Maybe it was Poplar. That's where I saw him the other day, the night he grabbed me. He was on Poplar." She felt desperate.

"We've checked every possibility. There is no Greg Leeds. No Greg Leeds at all. If he lives here then he doesn't drive or vote or pay utilities . . . " Scott ticked each item off on the fingers of his left hand. In the right he still held the voice recorder.

"I gave you his gun, remember?"

"It was *your* gun. Registered to *you*. Only *your* prints were on it."

"Winnie Tate!" she cried. "I was at the historical society with Greg. She saw us, she talked to him. She's the one who called you to come after me!"

"She said you were in there alone the day she called me. She said you were acting peculiar. Like you were talking to yourself. Not making sense," Scott said. "And then there's this journal you gave me. The one with all the information about Greg Leeds. The one that happens to be a journal purchased from The Rabbit Hole and written in your handwriting."

"Why are you doing this?"

"I'm not doing anything, Bess. I'm trying to figure out what's going on here." He clicked off the recorder and set it down on the coffee table. "Just . . . are you fucking with me?"

"Am I under arrest?"

"No, of course not. I don't understand what's going on. You've inserted yourself in an investigation you have no relation to. You're telling me the guy we arrested for it is no good and at the same time, you're sending me on a wild goose chase after a man who doesn't exist. It doesn't look good. Are you in some kind of relationship with Tam Gillis?"

"I can't believe you're even asking me that." Bess sat up quickly and regretted it immediately as her brain swam.

"I'm starting to feel like an idiot. And I don't like feeling like an idiot." His voice was harsh and cold. "I thought you were flirting with me this whole time and it never even occurred to me you were trying to . . . I don't know . . . throw me off. Distract me."

"I'm not. I'm not doing any of that."

"You've been using me and I can't figure out why."

"I want you to leave," Bess told him.

"I don't know if that's a good idea, Bess."

"I know my fucking rights. You can't be here if I don't want you. Are you charging me with a crime?"

"I could! I very well could! Obstructing justice would keep you tied up at least long enough for us to figure out what's happening." He studied her face for a moment, then added, "I don't know if you're well."

"It's Daniel Mills. He's got to you. He's making this all seem . . . He's doing this."

"I told you, I spoke with Mr. Mills. He was enormously polite. In fact, he spoke very highly of you. Why would he do that?"

"I don't know." Bess stood up slowly and stood still for a moment to steady herself before going to the refrigerator and pulling out a beer.

"Kinda early," Scott said.

She deliberately deepened her breaths. "Do you want one?"

"No, thanks."

"Suit yourself," she said and tipped the bottle up to her lips. "Scott, I want you to know something. It's really important to me." She strode back over to the couch and sat down next to him, closer this time, their arms touching, and faced him. "I haven't been playing with you. Not at all. I *was* flirting with you. The truth is, I haven't been able to stop thinking about you lately." She sipped her drink. "I'm not using you. Not in any way you wouldn't want me to." She leaned into him, her mouth stretching up toward his ear, and murmured, "How do you want me to use you, Scott?"

He leaned back and looked at her, a mixture of caution and longing fighting for control of his features. "I like you, Bess. But I don't think this is a good idea. I don't know if I can trust you."

"Well, isn't that the funniest thing I've heard all month?" Bess laughed loud enough to startle herself. "This whole time I've been trying to decide if I can trust *you.*"

ANTIOCH

"Who is Greg Leeds?"

The tension in the room was palpable. Anxiety flapped against her ribcage, threatened to burst out and run rampant. She tried to drown it with beer.

"You know, Daniel Mills talked to me about Jesus the other day and I can't get the fucking shit out of my head. He said maybe Jesus wasn't the Son of God. Maybe he's the actual antichrist we've all been so worried about for the last few centuries." She finished the bottle, went for another. "And I thought he was just . . . trying to distract me. I thought this was his great red herring to confuse me. But the more I think about it, the more sense it makes. And the more sense it makes, I start to wonder, is Daniel the Devil at all? Is the Dragon the Devil? Does the Devil tell us lies, or does he tell us our perfect truths? God damn, Scott. It's interesting, you know, when you think about it."

Scott didn't say anything, he picked up the recorder and pushed the record button once again. Not trying to hide it, right out in the open for her to see.

"If we've had the idea of good and evil twisted around all this time, what does that mean?" she asked.

"It doesn't mean anything, Bess. You know the difference between right and wrong."

"Do I? Do *you*?" Her voice rose slightly with each word.

"I think I do," he said, but she wasn't listening. Tears streamed down her cheeks, but she seemed to not notice.

"Animals don't have morality. Humans invented it with our big idiot brains. We decided our actions are right or wrong based on rules we made up ourselves and we still can't manage to agree or follow the rules. We stacked this deck and are still losing, Scott." Without warning, she flung her bottle hard against the garage door and screamed in genuine fright as it crashed and broke, scattering amber glass into the carpet.

Scott was up in a second, he wrapped his arms tight around her, pinning her arms to her sides. "Don't. Don't you hurt yourself," he told her.

"I don't know what's happening to me," she screamed.

"You're going to be okay. I swear." He loosened his grip. "I'm not going to let anything happen to you." He kissed her forehead, so soft it was barely a kiss at all.

"Please stay with me."

"I will."

He led her back into her bedroom. The floor was littered with crumpled clothes, notebooks, and loose papers. The bed itself was a bare mattress, all the sheets and blankets were pushed off to the floor. He pulled a soft fleece blanket from the heap and smoothed it over the bed. Bess lay down and he carefully removed her sneakers and covered her with a worn green quilt. Scott turned and started out of the room, but Bess caught his hand and tugged him back toward her.

"Stay," she said.

He left his own black dress shoes on as he slid into the bed next to her. She curled into his warmth, no longer caring if he was dangerous, just wanting to feel the comfort of his body against hers.

ANTIOCH

The room was empty when Bess awoke. She went to the bathroom and then searched the rest of her small home. Scott Howland was gone. Retrieving her phone from the kitchen counter she called him. It clicked straight to voicemail.

Bess checked the clock and saw that it was nine at night but had no idea what day it was. She'd lost time before. She tried Scott again. When his voicemail clicked on she hung up, not bothering to leave a message. She searched the counter and coffee table for a note but didn't find any. Going into the garage she saw nothing but her broken radio and felt a twinge of pain somewhere down inside of her soul. She pushed it away. There wasn't time for regret or sorrow. Not now.

The events of the last few days ran through her mind, jumbled, reordered, made themselves clear. She knew there was only one thing left for her to do. She hadn't made it to Mills's house the other night. Greg had distracted her. Scott said he saw Daniel at work, not his home. It was time someone paid him a visit.

Bess changed into jeans and a tee shirt, not bothering with a hoodie or her other stealth clothing from the night before. She didn't need to hide from anyone anymore. There was no point.

It was a twenty-minute walk from her front door to the river and just a few more minutes over to Poplar Street where Daniel Mills lived. She heard a

205

siren in the distance and wondered if someone was being saved. The pavement was wet from a recent shower and the air smelled like hot rain and nostalgia.

The sidewalk was cracked and broken. Dandelions poked up through cracks in the sidewalk and Bess avoided them for no particular reason. All the houses here were the same, identical white concrete slab homes sandwiched together with identical debris littering in their identical yards. Bess had written the address on the side of her hand and she checked the numbers. 224 Poplar Street. She was standing right in front of it.

The lot was small and the backyard was surrounded by a rundown wooden privacy fence that was probably once a golden brown, but had faded out to grey. A "Beware of Dog" sign on the gate hung slightly askew, but Bess did not hear any signs of an animal. The house was completely dark and Bess stepped onto the lawn.

There was a sudden clatter from inside the house, like a door flinging open and the subsequent rattling of poorly anchored furniture and knickknacks as it crashed back into its frame. Bess dashed over to the fence and pressed herself against it as flat as possible. Sucking in, trying to be small.

A man burst from the front door and landed on the lawn like a cougar, slowly rising, sniffing, looking for prey. Bess held her breath and prayed to a god she didn't believe in to keep her safe, keep her hidden, keep her secrets. Slowly the man moved away from the house and down the street, stopping to survey the area, searching still for the force that disturbed it.

Once he was out of sight, Bess peeled herself away

from the fence and crept back into the yard. She reached the stone path leading to the house and waited, listening. There was a soft shuffling noise behind her, like sneakers on gravel, and she turned to look.

A man stood on the opposite side of the street. Someone Bess did recognize. He stood, illuminated beneath a street light. Greg Leeds stared at her, a small smile on his lips. The house was right there, but she knew she'd never see the inside. She had to follow Greg, her own personal white rabbit.

Greg didn't move as Bess jogged over to him. He did not turn to smoke or fade away like she expected a ghost to.

"Why do they think you aren't real?" she asked him.

"You can't be here," Greg said.

"You're too late, I already am."

Greg stepped back into the grass and out of the lamplight. "You have to go home, Bess. He'll be waiting for you there."

"Who's waiting for me?"

"Don't let yourself be caught here. He's waiting."

She looked back toward the house, knowing it was the answer, but also that maybe it wasn't her question.

ANTIOCH

BESS'S HOME WAS lit up like she was having a party. Had she left all the lights on? She couldn't remember and it didn't matter. Her door was unlocked and that didn't matter either.

Inside the house her garage door was open and maybe she did that herself. Maybe she left it open when she was leaving. She could have. She was there. But the smashed radio was no longer on the floor, and that she did not do. The battered, broken radio was on the table once more, yet somehow it was alive— turned on and humming with static that reverberated through the room. She didn't spend time wondering how this was possible. All things were possible through the Dragon.

With great reverence, like a nun entering a church, she crossed the threshold of the garage and sat (knelt) before her radio. Bess did not bother to tune the radio, it would not be necessary. He was waiting for her and he would find her.

ANTIOCH

You've done so well.

The deep, masculine voice she associated with the Dragon purred through the speaker.

Don't worry, Margaret. It's almost over now.
You did these things because you wanted to. And I'm proud of you.

"I didn't do anything," Bess said.

You've been faithful and good. Poor Bess. Unloved by a father who can't bear the memories you represent. Unloved by a fiancé who put others before you and strayed. Unloved by the friends who abandoned you. But I love you, Bess Jackson. And my love is eternal.

There was a shrill, deafening screech from the radio and Bess clapped her hands over her ears.

When Bess awoke she knew there was someone else in the room. The air had a heavy recycled feeling. She sat up slowly, being careful of the crick in her neck, and stretched her arms over her head. Her cheek was cold from being pressed against the concrete floor.

"I know you're here," she told the room. The only

209

response was a long slow exhale from somewhere behind her.

Bess turned around and saw a slender figure standing in the open doorway between her garage and living room. Long blond hair hung limp down to the shoulders, weighted down by grease and dirt.

"Amy?" Bess asked.

The figure turned away and walked in toward her kitchen. Bess stood and followed her. The woman was in front of the kitchen counter now, looking back at Bess. She wore nothing but a long dirty white tee shirt with light rust-colored stains on it.

"Amy, is that you?" Bess asked.

"Stay away from me," the woman said.

Bess stepped forward. "Amy, you don't have to be afraid. I'm not going to hurt you."

The woman was crying now, crouched down, her arms covering her head. "Please, I'm sorry," she wailed. "I swear I didn't know. He told me he was single. I didn't know."

"You don't understand," Bess said. "I'm not who you think I am. Everything's going to be okay." She bent down over the sobbing woman and reached out to soothe her.

Something struck her, hard on the back of the head. Bess collapsed to her knees, her mind racing. She tried to turn, to see who was behind her, but another solid hit came down and then all was white and then, finally, peacefully, black.

ANTIOCH

Bess's eyes fluttered open and her right hand instinctively reached for her head. It was sticky with dried blood. Lifting herself onto her elbows, she looked around the room and found it empty. She stood up, but a hard wave of dizziness and nausea overtook her immediately and she fell back to her knees, retching hot bile onto the carpet.

The loud knock on the door would normally have startled her, but now it sent fresh agony tearing through her skull.

"Help," she called as loud as she could manage, hoping it was enough. "I need help."

The door wasn't locked and Detective Scott Howland was in the house in a matter of seconds.

"Bess," he cried. "What happened?" Before she could even think of an answer he was talking to someone else. "I need an ambulance at 1976 Glass Street. Blunt trauma to the head, single victim."

"Amy," Bess said, struggling to stay conscious. "Amy was here. She escaped or . . . " She trailed off, not knowing how to finish the thought.

"Shhhh. Don't worry about that now. Help is on the way," he told her. He crouched down next to her, careful to avoid the small puddle of vomit soaking into the carpet. A chill went through Bess's body as she felt his arm slide around her shoulders.

"No, we have to find Amy." Staying conscious was a struggle. Her thoughts were disjointed.

"Don't worry about Amy. Just sit tight, help is on the way."

"Could still be here . . . " Bess shook her head to clear the cobwebs, but a scorching wave of nausea made her stop.

JESSICA LEONARD

"Bess, they already found Amy. Don't think about that now."

"Where was . . . ? Okay?" Bess asked.

Detective Howland was quiet for a few seconds then he muttered, "They found the head a couple blocks from here. No body yet."

Amelia Earhart crashed into the Pacific Ocean and drowned.

ACKNOWLEDGEMENTS

A novel can be many things. This novel in particular is a love story to all the people who supported and helped me along the way. I could not have done this without the love, friendship, support, feedback, and reassurance of the following people: Jonathan Taylor, Jamie Parkest, Josh and Tara Moyes, all the writers who've genuinely become friends, all the friends who've genuinely cared about my writing, Amelia Earhart, Max Booth III and Lori Michelle of Perpetual Motion Machine Publishing for giving this strange little book a chance—I am forever grateful. And most of all, my husband Sean who has believed in me and held my hand through all the highs and lows. Sean has been my proofreader and partner through everything, and he has all my love—always. Thank you, reader, for going on this journey with me. I hope it was fun.

ABOUT THE AUTHOR

Jessica Leonard lives in western Kentucky with her husband, son, and two dogs. *Antioch* is her first novel.

ABOUT THE AUTHOR

IF YOU ENJOYED *ANTIOCH*, DON'T MISS THESE OTHER TITLES FROM PERPETUAL MOTION MACHINE . . .

THE NIGHTLY DISEASE
BY MAX BOOTH III
ISBN: 978-1-943720-24-8
$17.95

Sleep is just a myth created by mattress salesmen. Isaac, a night auditor of a hotel somewhere in the surreal void of Texas, is sick and tired of his guests. When he clocks in at night, he's hoping for a nice, quiet eight hours of Netflix-bingeing and occasional masturbation. What he doesn't want to do is fetch anybody extra towels or dive face-first into somebody's clogged toilet. And he sure as hell doesn't want to get involved in some trippy owl conspiracy or dispose of any dead bodies. But hey . . . that's life in the hotel business. Welcome to The Nightly Disease. Please enjoy your stay.

LIKE JAGGED TEETH
BY BETTY ROCKSTEADY

ISBN: 978-1-943720-21-7

$12.95

The guys following her home are bad enough, but when Jacalyn's Poppa comes to the rescue, things only get worse. After all, he's been dead for six years. There's no time to be relieved, because when she ends up back at Poppa's new apartment, nothing feels right. The food here doesn't taste how food should taste. The doors don't work how doors are supposed to work. And something's not right with Poppa. Guilt and sickness spiral Jacalyn into a nightmarish new reality of Lynchian hallucinations and grotesque body horror.

THE GIRL IN THE VIDEO
BY MICHAEL DAVID WILSON
ISBN: 978-1-943720-43-9
$12.95

TELL ME WHAT YOU LIKE.

After a teacher receives a weirdly arousing video, his life descends into paranoia and obsession. More videos follow—each containing information no stranger could possibly know. But who's sending them? And what do they want? The answers may destroy everything and everyone he loves.

The Perpetual Motion Machine Catalog

Baby Powder and Other Terrifying Substances | John C. Foster | Story Collection

Bleed | Various Authors | Anthology

Bone Saw | Patrick Lacey | Novel

Born in Blood Vol. 1 | George Daniel Lea | Story Collection

Crabtown, USA: Essays & Observations | Rafael Alvarez | Essays

Dead Men | John Foster | Novel

Destroying the Tangible Issue of Reality; or, Searching for Andy Kaufmann | T. Fox Dunham | Novel

The Detained | Kristopher Triana | Novella

Gods on the Lam | Christopher David Rosales | Novel

Gory Hole | Craig Wallwork | Story Collection

The Green Kangaroos | Jessica McHugh | Novel

Invasion of the Weirdos | Andrew Hilbert | Novel

Last Dance in Phoenix | Kurt Reichenbaugh | Novel

Like Jagged Teeth | Betty Rocksteady | Novella

Live On No Evil | Jeremiah Israel | Novel

Long Distance Drunks: a Tribute to Charles Bukowski | Various Authors | Anthology

Lost Films | Various Authors | Anthology

Lost Signals | Various Authors | Anthology

Mojo Rising | Bob Pastorella | Novella

Night Roads | John Foster | Novel

Quizzleboon | John Oliver Hodges | Novel

The Ritalin Orgy | Matthew Dexter | Novel

The Ruin Season | Kristopher Triana | Novel

So it Goes: a Tribute to Kurt Vonnegut | Various Authors | Anthology

Standalone | Paul Michael Anderson | Novella

Stealing Propeller Hats from the Dead | David James Keaton | Story Collection

Tales from the Holy Land | Rafael Alvarez | Story Collection
Tales from the Crust | Various Authors | Anthology
The Girl in the Video | Michael David Wilson | Novella
The Nightly Disease | Max Booth III | Novel
The Tears of Isis | James Dorr | Story Collection
The Train Derails in Boston | Jessica McHugh | Novel
The Writhing Skies | Betty Rocksteady | Novella
Time Eaters | Jay Wilburn | Novel
Touch the Night | Max Booth III | Novel
We Need to Do Something | Max Booth III | Novella

Patreon:
www.patreon.com/pmmpublishing

Website:
www.PerpetualPublishing.com

Facebook:
www.facebook.com/PerpetualPublishing

Twitter:
@PMMPublishing

Newsletter:
www.PMMPNews.com

Email Us:
Contact@PerpetualPublishing.com

9 781943 720491